CURSES AND COUSINS

HELEN VIVIENNE FLETCHER

FAMILIAR MAGIC SERIES READING ORDER

Familiars and Foes

Accidents and Apparitions (Published in *Jingle Spells*)

Curses and Cousins

CHAPTER ONE

deline stretched, feeling her feet peek out at the end of the quilt. In a second, Coco had found them and was licking between her toes.

She squirmed away. "Stop it, puppy!" He flopped down, propping his head on her knee instead.

Adeline lay back, delighting in how amazingly comfortable her couch was. She never thought she'd hear herself say that but being able to scooch up against the cushions while she slept had become more and more appealing as Bump had grown.

Speaking of Bump, she knew she wouldn't be able to lie there much longer, as the baby had shifted, pressing against her bladder. Adeline gently moved her hand across her stomach, marvelling at the rounded surface of it. As if feeling her touch, Bump kicked, right into her palm.

I'm here, Mum! her baby seemed to say.

Adeline drew her hand away, anxiety clutching at her

chest suddenly. She was going to be a mum… how was that possible when she barely felt like an adult herself?

"Hey there, sleepyhead." Hemi poked his head around the doorframe, and she peered up at him, anxiety dissipating at the sight of his smile.

Her plan had been to nap after work so that by the time he got home for his dinner break, she'd be refreshed and ready to hang out. It seemed she hadn't quite made that work, but the upside was a delicious smell floated through from the kitchen now. Waking up in time for dinner wasn't quite as good as waking up in time to welcome him home, but it had meant she'd slept through the prep and cooking time. She couldn't say she was mad about that.

Adeline waited for Hemi to join her on the couch. Instead, he leaned back against the doorframe, the corners of his lips curling up as he watched her.

"What?"

His grin grew. "I'm waiting for you to announce you need to pee and race off to the bathroom."

Adeline threw a cushion at him. "I don't *always* need to pee when I wake up from a nap." Bump kicked Adeline's bladder as if accusing her of lying, and Adeline glanced at her stomach. *Siding with Daddy already, are you?*

"Oh yeah?" Hemi stepped towards her. "So… there'd be no problem if I decided to tickle you right now?"

"No!" Adeline shot up, laughing before he even touched her. "Don't you dare!"

Hemi caught her around her waist, but he didn't tickle

her, pulling her in for a kiss instead. She settled her head against his chest for a moment, delighting in the warmth of him.

"Dammit," she whispered.

"What?" Hemi pulled back to look at her.

"This is the best hug, but I really *do* need to pee."

Hemi chuckled. "Go on. I'll be here when you get back." He gave her one last squeeze then let go, pushing her towards the bathroom.

Coco got up, following Adeline. He'd always been her little shadow, but he'd been sticking particularly close lately. Adeline tried not to worry it meant something was wrong.

Hemi was sitting on the couch when Adeline returned to the living room. He reached out an arm, and she curled up next to him, automatically placing one of the patch-work couch cushions on her lap. Bump was becoming more and more obvious, and she found herself hiding behind things. Up until now, Adeline's stomach had only *just* been big enough to be called a bump, small enough that Adeline and Hemi hadn't told anyone yet, and disguisable with well-draped clothes (and a touch of magic). Adeline hadn't even told her cousin, though she suspected with Clara's witchy powers, her cousin had probably picked up on something before they even knew themselves.

Hemi had been keen to tell his family at Christmas, but Adeline was too superstitious for that. Besides, they'd only found out on Christmas Eve themselves. Adeline had insisted they wait, though with every day there was more of a risk that Coco would give them away. Her assistance dog had been obsessed with Adeline's stomach, as had Clara's guide dog, Lola. She supposed it was to be expected – being both assistance dogs and familiars gave them a ridiculous amount of insight into everything around them.

At least Adeline's workmates hadn't figured it out. They'd put her tiredness down to her usual health problems, something Adeline was both relieved and irritated by. She felt like she was eleven months pregnant already. Hopefully, she'd get a second wind at some point, otherwise Hemi would be living with sleeping beauty for the rest of her pregnancy.

"How's your shift going?" she asked.

"So-so. Nothing terrible." Hemi tossed one of Coco's well-chewed soft toys off the couch. Coco pounced on it, taking it over to his bed.

Hemi didn't look at Adeline, and there was a hesitancy in the way he spoke. Was he keeping something from her? She forced herself to relax. Most likely, he'd attended an emergency with an epileptic patient, or a pregnant woman, and didn't want to upset her. She didn't press it.

"So…" Hemi said.

There it was again – perhaps his hesitancy wasn't related to his ambulance service shift after all.

"My cousin might be coming to visit," he said finally.

Adeline brightened. "Oh, exciting! Which one?"

Strangely, Hemi didn't seem to share her excitement. "Mimi," he said.

Adeline frowned. "Which one is Mimi?" Adeline didn't think she'd been at Christmas, but then again, there had been so many members of Hemi's family crowded into the house, it would have been easy to forget one. Adeline had been in hospital Christmas Eve, not to mention just finding out about the pregnancy, so she hadn't exactly been the perfect host.

"She came to live with my parents for a while when we were teenagers. Remember?" he said.

Adeline had a vague memory of an older girl staying in Hemi's guestroom, but the girl had been sulky, not wanting anything to do with two annoying thirteen-year-olds. She didn't think Mimi had said two words to either of them.

"Okay…" Adeline hoped she didn't sound too unenthusiastic; Hemi's family were always welcome in their home, sulky or not.

Coco settled down next to Adeline's feet, watching the conversation. His eyes flicked back and forth between Adeline and Hemi as if he were taking in every word, which to be fair, he probably was. Hemi reached out, patting Coco's head, and his tail flicked happily against Adeline's feet.

"She's been living in Nana Tui's old place up in Hastings, but she needs somewhere to stay down here. It will only be for a couple of weeks, I promise."

Adeline shook her head. "She's family. As long as she

doesn't mind living with a fat potato, she can stay as long as she likes."

A familiar deep dimple appeared in Hemi's cheek as he grinned. "A beautiful potato." He leaned over to plant a kiss on Adeline's lips.

Adeline blushed, even though she didn't feel particularly beautiful right now. Not with her nap-mussed hair and puffy cheeks. "Is she moving to Wellington?"

Hemi frowned again. "No…" He shook his head. "I'm not exactly sure of the details. Mum just said she was having some trouble."

Adeline had a vague memory that that was the reason she had come to stay with his family when they were younger as well, though she suspected that had been more teenage drama than actual trouble. Coming to stay as an adult was different.

Hemi sighed. "Anyway, I've been waiting ages for you to wake up, so we can have dinner."

Adeline clucked her tongue. "So demanding, insisting I wake up to eat this beautiful meal you've just prepared."

Hemi pulled Adeline to her feet, and Coco leapt up with them, hopeful as ever that there might be some food in it for him.

Mimi was due to arrive at two o'clock, so Adeline and Coco left the office at one thirty the next day. They passed

Kate Sheppard's ghost on the way home, outside her namesake apartments. The spirit gave Adeline a nod, which she returned, then Kate drifted away, disappearing as she did. Adeline smiled. Her hometown felt friendlier now the ghosts could see her too. She still hadn't heard Kate speak, but she supposed even the nod was fairly new for both of them.

Adeline arrived home at five to two, which of course left her flustered. Not being early was late in her books. It seemed Mimi didn't subscribe to the same philosophy, though. She hadn't arrived by the time Hemi had to leave for his shift, and it was nearly four o'clock when Adeline finally heard a knock on the door.

Naturally, after sitting alone on the couch for more than half an hour, Adeline had fallen asleep again. That seemed to be her main status of being at the moment. Coco, of course, was on high alert. He raced to the door, dashing back and forth a few times to let her know that there was someone there. Before she could get herself off the couch, another knock sounded, and Adeline made a half-hearted attempt at jogging over to it.

She opened the door. Even if Adeline hadn't been expecting Hemi's cousin, she would have known the woman on the doorstep was his family. She had deep brown eyes, just like Hemi's, and flawless, warm skin.

"Adeline?"

Adeline nodded. "You must be Mimi."

Adeline was surprised to find she felt nervous. Nervous, and frumpy. Mimi wore a flowing dress in a beautiful mix of swirling blues and purples, perfectly matched with a large blue and silver pendant necklace. Her long curly hair was pulled back with an old, red dress tie. The effect was somewhat marred by the fact that the tie still had the label attached, a yellow tag peeking out from behind her ear, denoting that it was made by some men's fashion company. Still, she looked gorgeous.

In contrast, Adeline had changed into leggings and one of Hemi's hoodies after work, and her hair, still growing out from her awful bob-cut decision last year, probably stuck out in all directions after the nap. Adeline knew she was accepted in Hemi's family, but somehow nerves still popped out their heads every time she met someone new, just in case they took an instant dislike to her and warned Hemi off her forever. Fortunately, Coco had none of those qualms and squeezed his way between Adeline's legs to present Mimi with a stuffed elephant.

Mimi dropped down into a crouch, smooshing Coco's head between her hands. "Oh, aren't you the cutest little thing!"

Coco's tail went into double-time wagging in delight.

"Come on in," Adeline said.

Mimi looked up at her and Adeline had a sense she was just as nervous about meeting a new person as Adeline was. "Thanks," she said. "Is Hemi here?"

Adeline shook her head. "He's on a late shift, unfortunately. You're stuck with me."

Mimi gave a forced laugh. "All good." She leaned down to pick up her bag.

The setting sun caught Adeline's eye as Mimi shifted, and she raised a hand to shield her eyes. For a moment, she couldn't see anything, then Adeline gasped as her pupils dilated and her sight returned. A wispy figure had appeared behind Mimi, during Adeline's moment of blindness. The wisps took shape, coiling strands of smoke becoming a man with a thin moustache and receding hairline.

Adeline glanced at Mimi. She didn't seem aware of the ghost behind her.

The spirit looked around, his gaze seeming to pass straight through Adeline. Then he whispered something, the sound coming out as a hiss. Adeline shivered, cold suddenly.

His gaze fell on Mimi, and he slithered towards her. He leaned forward, his whispering smoky lips just beside Mimi's ear. He reached out a hand as if to wrap it around her neck.

"Don't!" Adeline stepped forward, putting herself between the ghost and Hemi's cousin.

Mimi looked up, startled. The ghost disappeared, leaving behind a single smoky strand brushing across Mimi's throat.

Adeline blinked. Her heart raced, and it took her a moment to find words. "Let me help you with that," she said, reaching for Mimi's bag as if that had been her plan all along.

Mimi shook her head. "No, that's okay. I got it."

Adeline shook her head too, trying to clear it. "Come

on in," she said again, eager to get Mimi inside and close the door on the ghost.

Adeline showed Mimi upstairs to the room she and Hemi had set up the night before. The ghost didn't reappear, and Adeline tried to shake the unsettled feeling it had left her with. Spirits were mostly harmless, she reminded herself. But still, she couldn't get the thought of those transparent fingers wrapping around Mimi's neck out of her head.

Mimi glanced around the spare room, and Adeline was disconcerted to find she couldn't read Mimi's expression. Was she disappointed? She would have to take what she got, given she'd arrived without much notice.

Mimi dropped her bag on the bed, her whole body seeming to sag with the movement. "Do you mind if I take a nap?" she asked. "It was a long drive down here."

Adeline smiled. A woman after her own heart. "Of course. I'll be downstairs if you need anything."

Adeline closed the door gently behind herself and turned to go back downstairs. A flicker of smoke caught her eye. She glanced back towards Mimi's door, but whatever it was disappeared when she looked directly at it.

"Hello?" she called.

Nothing moved in response. Her ancestors stared down from their sepia-toned photos on the wall, watching, but remaining firmly in their frames. Adeline shifted, making the wooden floorboards creak under her feet.

"Do we need to worry, puppy?" she asked Coco.

She expected him to look up at her, his back-end wiggling in his own little happy dance. Instead, he stared into the space where the smoke had been as if waiting for it to reappear. Adeline stared too, seeing nothing but thin air.

CHAPTER TWO

Mimi didn't re-emerge from her room, and Adeline was left wondering if she should head up there and knock on the door to let her know dinner was ready. In the end, she decided to take Hemi's lead and just let her sleep. Adeline didn't like being woken from a nap, even if it was for food, and she had a suspicion Mimi might feel the same.

Hemi would be getting dinner at work, but Adeline served out three portions of the pasta she'd made anyway. Even when he'd already eaten, she found he often wanted second dinner when he got home, especially if it was pasta.

Adeline had just settled down to eat when she heard a noise coming from upstairs. She turned around, expecting to see Coco halfway up the stairs. He had a habit of sleeping there and sometimes slid down a few steps when he rolled over, waking himself up. But Coco lay on the couch next to her, eyeing her pasta hopefully. She put her bowl down on the wooden chest that served as a coffee table and got up. "Mimi?" she called.

There was no answer from upstairs. Coco got up, nudging at the back of her knee. He peered up at her expectantly.

"Do you think we should go check on her?" she asked him.

He wagged his tail, agreeing with her.

Adeline took one last longing glance at her pasta, then made her way upstairs. Coco trotted along beside her.

Mimi's door was closed. Adeline knocked gently on it, hoping she wouldn't startle Mimi if she were asleep. There was no answer from inside. Adeline went to knock again when the tell-tale wisps of smoke started to form in the corridor. She glanced towards Coco, trying to gauge his reaction. He watched the ghost appear, his ears pricked back, alert, but not overly panicked.

The ghost's face started to form, swirls of smoke outlining hints of hair, nose, and eyes. Above the lips, she could see the suggestion of a thin moustache – the same ghost she'd seen on the doorstep.

"Excuse me… what do you want?" she asked him.

Once again, his eyes passed straight through her. Prior to a year or so ago, no ghosts had ever interacted with Adeline, but after all the drama she'd experienced with her great-great-grandfather, and the ghosts of her ancestors, Millie and Jenny, she'd gotten used to ghosts not only seeing her but coming up and chatting.

This one either couldn't tell she was there or just wasn't interested. He looked around, glancing down at his own hands as if surprised to see their smoky outlines. He raised his head, and Coco reached out to sniff him.

The ghost lurched forward, placing his hand on the door to Mimi's room.

"Wait!" Adeline yelled.

But the ghost was already gone. He disappeared through the wall into Mimi's room. Adeline held her breath, but there was silence from inside. She raised her hand to knock.

Mimi screamed.

"Mimi? Adeline called. She hammered on the door with her fist. "Mimi, are you okay?" Coco whimpered. He darted back and forth in the corridor, looking up at Adeline for reassurance.

A rustling came from inside, then Mimi opened the door. She still wore the floaty dress and the red tie, but it had slipped back, leaving her hair bedraggled. The room behind her stood empty, no sign of wisps or ghosts.

Mimi blinked at Adeline. "Sorry," she said then gave a half-laugh. "I guess I was in a deep sleep. Weird dreams."

Adeline forced a laugh in return. "Yeah…" She wasn't quite sure how to bring up the question of what Mimi had seen. *Hey, by the way, did you see a strange man walk through the wall just then?* wasn't exactly something she could ask without sounding crazy. She didn't want to scare Mimi any further.

Mimi stared at her, and Adeline realised she had to say something, even if it wasn't about the ghosts.

"Now you're awake, I've made some pasta if you want some?"

Mimi hesitated, and for a moment Adeline was sure she was going to say no. Then Mimi's stomach rumbled, and her expression turned sheepish. "Yeah, thanks. I'm starving." Mimi moved as if to join Adeline in the corridor, then she glanced back into her room. "Oh – I nearly forgot, I have a present for you. A 'thank you' for letting me stay." Mimi disappeared inside.

Adeline blinked, taking a second to shift gears from ghosts to gifts. "That's so kind. You didn't have to do that."

There was another lot of rustling, then Mimi returned, holding a glass jar. "It's nothing. Hemi said you like honey." She held out the jar, flushing slightly as if suddenly unsure of the present.

Adeline took it and gave Mimi a warm smile. "I do – thank you so much, it's lovely." The jar felt warm in her hand, almost as if Mimi's good intentions were wrapped around it.

Mimi returned the smile with a more hesitant one. Adeline couldn't help noticing that Mimi's face still held some tension, and she knew she would have to bring up the question of ghosts at some point. She also knew from experience; these things were a lot easier to deal with on a full stomach.

She tilted her head towards the stairs. "Come on, let's

get some food. Just don't let Coco fool you into giving him any. He's had his dinner. He's just a Labrador."

Coco wagged his tail, recognising they were talking about him. Adeline watched him carefully, but his earlier fear had dissipated now Mimi was standing next to them. He danced around her, as she walked down the corridor, just happy to have all the humans in the same room. Adeline waited until Mimi turned towards the stairs then did a quick check of the room. No wisps of smoke or ghostly outlines appeared. The spirit was well and truly gone.

"Very strange," she said to herself.

Dinner was more awkward than Adeline had expected. Mimi flicked on the light in the dining room, before Adeline could stop her, and she couldn't think of a way to turn it off again without seeming passive aggressive. Normally, Adeline lit this space with lamps rather than the main light, giving it a warm cosy feel. Fully illuminated, the room loomed around them – the dark wood of the walls and floor making the space imposing.

Adeline guessed it would have been considered grand once, but now shadows fell in odd places, giving the impression of memories trapped in time. More often than not, she and Hemi ate in the kitchen or on the couch instead.

The ghost had clearly unsettled Mimi, and she jumped at every creak – not exactly ideal when they lived in an old house. Adeline's reassurances didn't seem to help.

"Hemi said you were living at your nan's place before this?"

Mimi looked up, her eyes widening, and Adeline couldn't help feeling she'd said something wrong, but she had no idea what.

"I mean he just mentioned it in passing… he didn't really say anything else." Had that been a secret? Surely Hemi would have told her if it was something she wasn't supposed to talk about.

Mimi dropped her gaze again. "Yeah, I was living there for a while. I moved in to help Nana Tui out when she got sick, then just stayed on."

"That was kind of you."

Mimi's eyes flicked to meet Adeline's, and there was a hint of alarm in them.

Adeline frowned. "Looking after your nan, I mean. That was a really lovely thing to do for her. Very kind." Adeline stumbled through the explanation.

Mimi shifted uncomfortably. "I was close to Nana Tui. It seemed like the right thing to do." Somehow, Mimi's words didn't quite match her tone.

"So, what brought you to Wellington?"

Mimi shrugged. "Nothing in particular. Just a visit." She rubbed her eyes, and Adeline couldn't tell if it was out of tiredness or a desire not to make eye contact.

"You're always welcome here. I'm sure Hemi and I can

show you around on his day off. There's some beautiful sights in the city."

"Thanks, that's nice of you, but…" Mimi shifted uncomfortably. "I'll probably do my own thing. I'm just not that into sightseeing."

Adeline felt herself blush a little. "Sure. Of course."

"Besides, I need to go talk to some real estate developers. I'm thinking of selling the house."

It was Adeline's turn to look up suddenly, surprised. "Nana Tui's house?"

"Yeah."

Adeline had only visited Hemi's nan's house once or twice, when they were teenagers, but she remembered it being a magical place. It had been painted in bright colours and had plants hanging from the ceiling in every room, along with crystals and colourful ornaments. To Adeline, it had been like stepping into a fairyland.

She remembered Hemi's mother shaking her head and laughing about the state of things. That had made Adeline even more determined that that's what her house would look like when she grew up. Obviously, she'd let go of that dream, but a part of her wondered if it just meant that she wasn't done growing up yet. Maybe someday her house would look exactly like Nana Tui's.

"Wow, that a big decision." Adeline wasn't sure if that was rude to say, but it was – a *very* big decision, and she was surprised Mimi was talking about it so casually.

Mimi just shrugged in response. Adeline had no claim to the house, of course, but the thought of it being sold to a developer made her stomach twist. She let the silence hang for a moment, giving Mimi the opportunity to say more if she wanted, but not pressing the issue. Instead, Mimi seemed to grow uncomfortable in the silence. She took out her phone, scrolling through her messages as she ate.

Adeline picked up her fork, focusing on her food. "Not bad, eh, puppy?" she said. "Not as good as Dad's pasta, but I think we did okay."

Coco wagged his tail in response.

Mimi shot her a confused look, and Adeline blushed again. "Sorry, I normally talk to Coco when I'm here by myself."

Mimi raised an eyebrow. "And does he answer?"

Adeline glanced down at Coco, who had taken up residence on her feet. Mimi would be surprised as to what he could do.

They spent the rest of the meal in silence. Eventually, Mimi excused herself, her pasta only half eaten. She headed back upstairs and shut herself in her room again. Adeline had to admit, she was relieved.

Hemi's ambulance shift didn't finish until the early hours of the morning, but Adeline stayed up anyway. After all, she had spent half the afternoon asleep on the couch. She made a half-hearted attempt at tidying up, which mostly meant moving Coco's soft toys into a pile while he watched on suspiciously from his bed.

Really, the place needed a good vacuum. Adeline had been sewing lately – hand stitching a patchwork quilt for her baby, just as her ancestors had done. Little scraps of fabric and thread kept getting caught between the floor-boards, and the room was now flecked with colour. Adeline secretly liked it. She preferred her home to feel lived in rather than sterile.

As predicted, Hemi's face lit up when he arrived home and saw she'd left pasta for him. He didn't even bother to get changed first, heating up the pasta and settling down on the couch next to Adeline in his paramedic uniform.

Adeline moved her quilt aside, grabbing the old red and brown blanket from the back of the couch instead and putting it over his lap.

Hemi stared at it, puzzled. "Am I cold?"

"In case you spill." More realistically, in case *she* spilled. She did not want to be responsible for accidentally tipping pasta into his lap and staining his uniform. "Besides," she added, tucking herself in next to him. "*I'm* cold and you can't cuddle while you're eating."

He grinned and kissed her temple. A cosy, happy, warmth spread through Adeline, which had nothing to do with the blanket.

"Did Mimi arrive okay?" he asked.

Adeline nodded. "Yes, she's upstairs asleep." At least, Adeline hoped Mimi was able to sleep, if the ghost hadn't freaked her out too much.

Hemi frowned. "Is everything okay?" he asked.

He could always tell when something was up. Adeline's plan to let him finish his dinner before explaining went out the window, as he read the tension on her face.

Adeline shrugged. "I'm not sure. There was a ghost."

Hemi nodded, used to this type of admission from Adeline.

She hesitated, wondering how to explain. "It didn't seem to see me, but I think..." She wasn't sure about this, but it had seemed like the ghost had followed Mimi here. Most of the ghosts she saw didn't really seem to be interested in people, or even places. They were like memories, manifestations of people following the routines they'd had in life – usually things that had been important to them or made them happy.

"It seemed like maybe Mimi could see it," Adeline said finally.

Hemi took a breath, and then another mouthful of pasta. Adeline frowned. She was used to low-key reactions from him; it was one of the things she loved about him. He'd been amazing at rolling with the supernatural parts of her life, but this was a little blasé even for him.

"You don't seem surprised," she said finally.

Hemi made a noise in his throat. "No, I am," he said. "Or maybe I'm not. Mum kind of hinted there was something like this going on."

Adeline blinked. "Your mum told you Mimi sees ghosts?"

Hemi shook his head. "No, she told me Mimi thinks

she's cursed." He gave a half-laugh. "I didn't believe it, of course. Mum doesn't either. But I thought maybe… you know, with everything that's happened, that it was something supernatural."

That made sense. With all that they'd experienced over the last year, Adeline and Hemi had both started expanding their definitions of what was possible. A few years ago, Adeline hadn't even known witches were real, now she was a witch with an assistant dog familiar, and a long-lost cousin teaching her how to use her magic.

"I think that might have been why she suggested Mimi come stay with us," Hemi added.

"You mean she knows about…?"

"No, no. I haven't told her anything." Hemi reached out to touch Adeline's arm, reassuring her. "But she's intuitive like that, and after the ghosts her mum used to see, I think she might have got a sense that you weren't exactly…" He trailed off, and Adeline could tell he was struggling with the terminology.

"Weren't exactly unfamiliar with the supernatural?" she finished for him.

"Yes! That." He grinned at her.

"That makes sense." Relief filled her, knowing that Hemi's mum accepted her enough to send Mimi down here for help. How much help she would actually *be* was another question.

"What did Mimi say about it?" Hemi asked.

Adeline shook her head. "I didn't ask. She seemed kind of freaked out and I didn't want to make it worse."

"Fair enough." Hemi sighed. "I guess we just wait and see if it happens again? I'll try talking to her about it as well."

"Thanks."

Adeline suspected Mimi would be more comfortable talking to Hemi anyway. In the meantime, she'd just have to keep an eye on the ghost. Coco leaned his head on her knee as if to remind her he was there to keep an eye out too. Or perhaps, he was just trying to get closer to Hemi's pasta.

deline woke before her alarm the next morning, despite the late night. Hemi's phone buzzed on the nightstand, but he showed no signs of waking to pick it up. She checked the caller ID – his mum. It stopped ringing before she had a chance to answer it, and she set it back down, letting Hemi sleep. He could call her back later in the day, after he'd gotten some rest.

Mimi hadn't emerged from her room, so Adeline crept downstairs to let Coco out, trying to keep as quiet as possible. Naturally, she promptly tripped over Coco, as he came back in, and sent her breakfast crashing onto the tiled floor. Lucky Hemi was a heavy sleeper. Unfortunately, it turned out Mimi wasn't. She appeared in the kitchen a few minutes later, wearing a worn pair of pyjama pants and a faded hoodie. Her hair fell loose around her shoulders, no sign of the bright tie now, and a tangle of stray strands poked out from the back of her head as if they had spent the entire night gathering static electricity.

"Sorry, I didn't mean to wake you," Adeline said. "This one got under my feet. He wants his breakfast."

Mimi rubbed Coco's head. "It's a good thing you're cute, eh?" Coco wagged his tail recognising the praise, if not the admonishment accompanying it.

Adeline stooped to pick up the fallen bowl of porridge, but Mimi shook her head. "Here, let me. You feed this one."

"Thank you. I don't know why I'm so clumsy lately."

"All good. I drop things all the time too."

Adeline filled Coco's bowl, and Mimi made quick work of the clean-up – a good thing, as Coco would have been eager to "help" had the porridge been on the floor a moment longer.

"How did you sleep? At least before I woke you, I mean."

Mimi shrugged. "Okay." But dark circles shadowed her eyes.

"I thought I heard you up in the night?" Adeline asked.

Mimi frowned. "Sorry, I didn't realise I'd disturbed you." There was a hint of reproach to Mimi's voice, and Adeline shook her head.

"No, no… I didn't mean that. I was up late waiting for Hemi anyway. I just meant after you screamed…"

Mimi gave a half-laugh as if remembering. "That was nothing. I'm fine."

"Are you sure? Because—"

"I said I'm fine."

"Right, sorry."

Adeline fell quiet, as Mimi bristled. Perhaps it was too early for conversation anyway. She watched Coco chasing the last few biscuits around his bowl, his collar hitting it every so often letting out a clanging chime.

Mimi seemed to grow unsettled by the noise. She fiddled with the silver chain around her neck, then glanced at the kettle. "Mind if I make a coffee?"

Adeline glanced at the kettle herself. "Yeah, of course. I should have offered." Adeline wasn't a coffee drinker, and she often forgot the place caffeine held in other people's lives.

Mimi filled the jug, then flicked the switch. She hovered over it as if it needed supervision to boil. Adeline reached for a mug, laughing as she had to stand on tiptoes to clasp the handle when it was on the top shelf. Mimi glanced her way, frowning.

Adeline tried to curb her laughter. "The dangers of height difference," she said. "Hemi's the coffee addict."

Mimi just stared at her, and heat crept across Adeline's cheeks. Could Mimi not hear her, or did she simply think Adeline ridiculous? "He puts things away up high because he's tall," she added quietly.

Mimi's phone beeped, and Adeline turned away, busying herself with finding the coffee, as Mimi took it out of her pocket. Mimi hadn't had any trouble hearing the phone, so Adeline was definitely in camp ridiculous as to the explanation for Mimi's silence.

Adeline placed the coffee and sugar on the bench, leaving Mimi to get her own milk. The jug gurgled, the water sloshing in a final moment of furious boiling before the switch automatically flicked off.

Mimi didn't pick it up. She stared at her phone, her lips parting as if she would read the message aloud, but her face tightened into a frown.

Adeline stepped towards her, reaching out without thinking. "Is everything okay?" A string of unanswered messages filled Mimi's phone screen, this new one just the latest from the same contact.

Mimi started, shoving the phone into her pocket. She grabbed the mug Adeline had left on the bench for her, and sloshed water from the jug into it. The water hit the side of the mug and bounced, flying straight out the other side and onto Mimi's hand. "Dammit!"

Adeline turned on the cold water, pushing Mimi's hand underneath. "How bad is it? Do you want me to get Hemi?"

Mimi shook her head. "It's nothing. I just screw every blimming thing up when I'm tired." She stared at the clear liquid in the mug, almost as if she expected it to turn to coffee by sheer force of will.

"Here, let me." Adeline took the jug from her. It was pretty obvious this wasn't just about the caffeine, but making hot drinks was one of the easiest ways to bring soothing magic to a person. An intention and an action – Adeline spooned coffee into the mug and added sugar and water, all the while keeping a calming intention clear in her mind. Her magic flowed into the drink, bringing the intention to reality.

Mimi took the coffee, wrapping her hands around it. Instantly, her shoulders relaxed, her whole body seeming to calm. Perhaps this was where Adeline should have started, rather than trying to force Mimi to talk about something she clearly didn't want to.

"Thanks," Mimi said after a beat. "You make good coffee for a caffeine-free weirdo."

Adeline laughed, though she had a feeling it wasn't just her dislike of coffee that had Mimi calling her a weirdo. Adeline made herself a ginger tea, adding a spoonful of the honey Mimi had given her the night before.

"Thanks again for this," she said, gesturing to the jar. "It's lovely."

Mimi softened further at the praise. "You're welcome. I'm glad you like it."

Adeline wanted to hold the calm moment a little longer, but she caught sight of the clock on the stove and grimaced. "I'm going to need to head to work in a minute," she told Mimi.

Mimi nodded, engrossed in sipping from her mug. Adeline hesitated. Though the hot drinks had seemed to help, things still felt weird between them. She was on unstable ground with Mimi, but she wasn't sure how to steady it.

She did want to take Coco to the park before work, though, and she needed to hurry up if she was going to make that happen. "I'll see you this evening, then."

Mimi gave another absent nod. Adeline grabbed a banana to make up for the breakfast she'd dropped and headed upstairs to get changed. When she came out, Mimi was back in her room with the door closed.

Adeline slipped Coco's jacket over his head, and his tail wagging slowed like a pendulum coming to a halt. He looked up at her, his eyes solemn now he was in work mode.

"Shall we go to the park before work?" she asked him.

His tail swung back into motion at the word "park". Adeline put her own jacket on, adding a "don't notice" intention as she smoothed it over her stomach. The magic wouldn't work to disguise Bump for much longer, but she'd keep it up while she could.

She opened the front door and felt in her handbag for her sunglasses. Coco trotted out onto the doorstep. "One minute, puppy." Adeline's fingers explored the recesses of her handbag, but still no sunglasses. If only Coco could be trained to sniff them out.

Adeline caught sight of herself in the window, sunglasses on the top of her head. "Your mum is silly, isn't she, puppy?" she called.

She could just see Coco's bum around the side of the door, and his tail danced at the sound of her voice, but his head was down, investigating something.

Adeline dashed forward. "Coco, drop it!"

He looked up at her, wide puppy eyes innocent, despite the broken chicken bone at his feet.

Adeline grabbed it, wincing at the slimy texture of the remnants of meat combined with dog slobber. "Who left that here, eh? Not for doggies."

Finding bones on the pavement wasn't exactly an unusual occurrence – she'd made many a mad dash trying to stop Coco from swallowing them – but she'd not found one on her doorstep before. "I better be more careful, eh pup?"

Coco followed at Adeline's heels as she returned to the kitchen to drop the bone in the bin, then picked up her handbag again. She caught a glimpse of a wispy figure outside the front door.

"Hello?" she called.

The ghost didn't answer so she made her way outside. The figure took shape, becoming the man with the thin moustache. Adeline stepped back, raising her hand defensively, but the ghost didn't attack. He floated on the doorstep, the smoky outlines of his body disappearing before they reached his feet.

"Did you come here with Mimi?" she asked. "What do you want with her?"

He blinked, slowly, the patterns of smoky wisps shifting to create the movement. He didn't look at Adeline, simply staring into the house as if straight through her.

Adeline hesitated. He didn't seem in any hurry to go

inside. She glanced down at Coco. He sniffed the ghost, his posture curious rather than alarmed, then raised his head. He pulled gently on his lead, shuffling towards the stairs.

"Is it safe to leave him here?" she asked him.

Coco looked up at her, almost as if to nod.

"Okay, puppy. If you think he's all right, we'll go to the park."

Coco wiggled happily, and Adeline edged her way around the ghost and out onto the street. The spirit still made no move to go inside the house. Adeline hoped she was doing the right thing. He hadn't hurt Mimi, but he had certainly given her a fright. Adeline made a mental note to message Hemi about the ghost and her conversation with Mimi once she got to work.

Adeline and Coco walked down the road a little way, then something made her look back. Her stomach dropped. The ghost was not alone. It was too far away for Adeline to make out the details, but she could see the outlines of five or six figures standing outside her door.

She took a step back towards the house, but Coco didn't follow. He looked away from Adeline, staring in the direction of the park.

"Are you sure, Coco? Don't you think we should go back?"

Coco's tail wagged at the sound of her voice, but he didn't look at her. He pulled lightly on the lead, edging away from home.

Adeline sighed. The ghosts hadn't gone inside the

house. Instead, they were clustered together outside, seemingly deep in conversation. Again, this was unusual. The ghosts Adeline most often saw didn't acknowledge each other. When they had the last time, it was because her great-grandfather was interfering with the very fabric of the universe, trying to bring himself back from the dead.

Coco looked up at her, his posture relaxed. He gave another little tail wag as if to say, "everything's okay, Mum, I promise."

"Okay, pup. I trust you."

Perhaps the ghosts had all known each other when they were alive, and that's why they were gathering together now. As Adeline watched, the ghosts disappeared. She couldn't tell whether they'd gone inside the house, or just drifted away, disappearing into the air. She hoped it was the latter. Mimi didn't seem like she'd cope with another supernatural visit.

Coco gave another tug on his lead, pulling her towards the park.

"Okay," she told him.

Mimi hadn't exactly welcomed her help this morning and Hemi had said he would talk to her. She had to trust him and stop trying to solve every problem herself.

The day was surprisingly still, the Wellington wind easing off for once, and Adeline settled into the rhythm of her steps. Walking was a necessity for her, not having a driver's license, but it was also a kind of therapy. She always felt less stressed after she'd spent some time wandering the streets with her faithful companion.

Her mind drifted back to the chicken bone on her doorstep. She'd almost forgotten it, with the ghost appearing, but suddenly it struck her as strange. Who was sitting eating chicken on her porch? She chuckled at the thought of someone stopping there for a picnic.

Perhaps it had been Mimi, Adeline thought. She'd have to speak to her about not leaving rubbish where Coco could reach it.

Adeline's steps faltered. Wisps of smoke formed on the pavement in front of her, coiling and swirling around each other as they began to take shape. Adeline's earlier laughter died in her throat. She stepped back, pulling Coco close to her side.

Her insides twisted as she waited for the figure to become clear. The feeling made her throat tighten too. She was used to greeting the ghosts as friends, not anxiously waiting to see if they had a moustache.

Finally, she saw a face in the smoke. The outline of the author, Katherine Mansfield, took shape, coils of smoke forming her bob haircut.

"Oh, it's you!"

The words burst from Adeline, louder and with more excitement than she'd ever greeted the author before. Coco wagged his tail, recognising Adeline's cheerful tone.

The ghost ignored both of them, perhaps unhappy with Adeline's overly familiar welcome.

"I'm sorry…" Adeline said. "It's just you startled me."

Katherine didn't respond. She drifted down the road, like she always did, making her way towards the museum which preserved her childhood home. She disappeared into the air underneath the "Historic Places" sign, just as Adeline had seen her do many times before.

Adeline sighed. "It's not my day, is it, Coco? I've annoyed Mimi, I've annoyed Katherine Mansfield…"

Something about that statement struck Adeline as funny, and she chuckled, prompting a tail wag from Coco. "At least you still love me, eh? Who needs ghosts when I've got you?" She rubbed his head, and he danced on the spot.

The lack of sleep caught up with Adeline about midday. Her work friend, Dana, plied her with sugar, but Adeline knew that could only keep her awake for so long. At four o'clock, she found herself staring blankly at her boss, no idea of the question he'd just asked her. Fortunately, he just laughed and sent her home. Adeline apologised profusely, but he waved it away, still in dad mode, trying to make things easier for her.

She would have to be more careful about getting enough sleep. She'd been lucky in that her seizures had been reasonably under control throughout her pregnancy, but her blood pressure had been all over the place. She felt lightheaded as she walked up the stairs coming home that evening, and Coco seemed to be sticking particularly close – usually a sign that she wasn't well.

"It's okay, puppy. We're home now."

All she could think about was ordering takeaways and vegging out in front of the TV. She wasn't sure if that was entirely polite with a guest, but she was going to have to make it work.

There were no more bones on the doorstep, which Adeline was thankful for. She didn't quite have the energy to deal with them this evening. A windchime hung in the entryway though, and Adeline stared at it blankly. In her tired state, she almost wondered if it had been there all along and she had somehow never noticed it before. But this was Wellington, where the wind crashed against walls with an unmissable force, and a windchime definitely wouldn't go unnoticed.

It clinked in the light breeze now, making a peaceful, soothing sound. Adeline touched the metal of one of the pipes, feeling the hum of vibrations against her fingertips. A swirling pattern of blues and greens covered it, like a peacock feather. The pattern reminded her of the flowing dress Mimi had worn the day before.

"Let's leave it there for now, shall we?" she said to Coco.

It was a sweet idea from Mimi, but it would probably have to come down before it drove the neighbours nuts with a chaotic cacophony in a storm. Perhaps it would be best to let Mimi figure that out for herself.

Mimi wasn't home; nor was Hemi, though Adeline

hadn't been expecting him to be. Mimi had stacked the dishwasher, and it looked like she'd cleaned the benches too. Adeline could get used to having a houseguest if it meant coming home to a clean house every day.

She opened the fridge, staring at the contents without much enthusiasm. She supposed being home alone meant she could order takeaways after all, but it did leave her with the problem of whether to order something for Mimi. It was so strange having to try and navigate life around another person.

Adeline touched her stomach. Soon, she'd be navigating around another person who couldn't yet communicate with her…

The house felt oddly quiet. Coco's little snores bounced around the space, and nothing but silence echoed from behind Mimi's closed door. Adeline turned the TV on, but her vision blurred, and her mind wandered, only the occasional ad catching her attention, as the volume turned from conversational to shouting.

The glowing time on the microwave reflected onto the kitchen door, almost as if it was taunting her with the hours left until Hemi was due home.

Adeline woke suddenly. Coco lay curled up in the space behind her legs, one paw stretched out over her thigh. The

TV was off, and a note lay on the coffee table in front of her.

Coco told me I shouldn't wake you. Come give me a kiss in the morning. Love you xx

Adeline yawned. She was tempted to head upstairs now and crawl into bed next to Hemi, but he would probably have only just fallen asleep, and while she could have eased her way in without waking him, Coco bouncing up onto the bed wouldn't be as gentle.

Coco shifted as if he'd heard her, rearranging himself to lie heavily across her feet. *Stay there, go back to sleep*, he seemed to say.

Adeline's eyelids agreed, pulling her down into dreams. The jangling of the windchime outside had them shooting open again. Coco's ears flew up. Adeline pulled herself into a sitting position, but Coco shifted with her, leaning against her legs, pinning her to the couch.

The fur on the back of his neck rose. He watched the door, and his ears held their pricked posture, but he remained in place, weighing Adeline down. Adeline's heart played percussion on the inside of her rib cage, but she trusted his instincts more than her own. If he was telling her to stay put, she would stay put.

Everything was quiet, then something thumped against the door. The windchime jangled, smashing against the wall.

Coco growled. He ran to the door, then crouched low, his lips pulled back into a snarl. Adeline leapt up, following him. The moustached ghost she'd seen earlier stood in the hallway. Through the frosted glass, she saw something moving outside.

The ghost leaned down, beckoning to Coco. He reached out a hand as if to grab Coco's collar.

"Coco, come!" Adeline pulled him back.

The ghost raised his hand, pointing to the door. He whispered something and a growl grew in Coco's throat again. The windchime clattered, and Adeline imagined spirits swirling around outside.

"It's just the wind," Adeline said. She drew an intention into the words, layering protective magic around herself and Coco. Another ghost appeared beside the moustached spirit. The smoke swirled, creating the shape of a person, but a face never formed. It stepped towards Adeline, eyeless sockets peering straight through her. Adeline gasped, reeling back.

The moustached ghost lunged forward, grasping at Coco.

"It's just the wind," Adeline yelled, pouring all of her magic into the words. "Nothing but the wind."

The ghost dissolved mid-step, his shape turning into a rush of air. Coco barked, straining against her hold on him. Adeline pulled him back, shutting the two of them in the living room.

The jangle of chimes and thumps against the door rose to a peak, then stopped abruptly as if the ghosts had scattered. Something clattered on the stairs, and Adeline spun around, letting out a shriek.

"Hey, hey, it's just me." Hemi stepped forward from the

shadows and wrapped Adeline in a hug. Coco whined and nudged against their legs, pushing both of them back towards the stairs.

"Okay, good boy. Good boy." Adeline stared at the living room door, half waiting for a tendril of ghostly smoke to creep underneath it. None appeared, the ghosts apparently only interested in waking up the neighbourhood.

"What happened?" Hemi asked. Coco let out another little whimper.

"Ghosts," Adeline said, that being the only answer she could really give. Hemi pulled her in tighter, and she squeezed him back just as hard.

CHAPTER FOUR

*H*emi's phone woke them again the next morning. Adeline watched with half-closed eyes as he picked it up, glanced at the caller ID, then set it down again without answering.

He looked over at her and smiled when he saw she was awake. "I swear I told Mum I was on nights," he said. He pulled Adeline into a hug, and she curled up against him.

He buried his face in her hair. "I hate that you have to go to work now."

Not as much as Adeline hated it. She loved her job, but if she could have pulled a sickie and spent the day curled up in bed with him, that would have been bliss. Unfortunately, health problems and pregnancy meant sick leave was strictly reserved for days when she was actually sick. Though, with the lack of sleep lately, those were starting to become the norm.

"So, last night..." he said.

Adeline closed her eyes. She didn't want to spoil the moment by talking about ghosts, but Hemi did deserve a proper explanation. "I don't know. The ghost Mimi's brought with her… it's not good."

Hemi frowned. "Is it trying to hurt her?"

"Scare her, I think, though seems like Mimi slept through last night."

Hemi shook his head. "She was awake. She was pretty freaked out, but I told her to stay upstairs."

So, the ghost had got what it wanted, if scaring Mimi was its plan, of course. Though many people were scared of ghosts, Adeline had never seen one actively behave this way. On the rare occasion she'd come across one that wasn't harmless, they'd always had a motive beyond just trying to freak someone out. And why Mimi? What had she ever done to anyone? No wonder she'd imagined she was cursed if this is what she'd been dealing with.

Hemi drew his hands down his face. Making sense of ghostly behaviour was difficult at the best of times, and they were both exhausted.

"Are you okay?" he asked.

"Yeah, I'm—"

A scream from downstairs cut Adeline off. Coco leapt up from his bed on the floor. He raced across the room, clattering down the stairs. Adeline and Hemi followed him, seconds later.

Mimi stood in the hallway, staring out at the doorstep. Her whole body shook, and she held a trembling hand pressed to her lips.

Hemi wrapped his arm around her. "What is it? What's wrong?"

Coco dashed out the open door, and Adeline chased after him. He picked something up.

"Drop it!" Adeline yelled, grabbing his collar.

Coco spat out a black, glossy feather. Similar feathers littered the porch.

"Oh, a bird's got in." A sick feeling came over Adeline. Had the ghosts caused this? Had they coaxed the bird inside, only to leave it trapped, bashing around trying to find its way out?

"Is it still there?" Hemi asked.

Adeline nudged Coco back inside before checking. He was pretty gentle with small animals, but a large dog nose would hardly be comforting to a startled bird. She checked the corners of the entryway but saw no sign of anything living. "I think it's gone." She pulled a feather from between the pipes on the windchime. "It must have hit this, and then panicked." No wonder, with a ghost terrorising it.

"It hit the windchime," Mimi whispered. Her hands still shook, and she'd gone pale. She turned suddenly, yanking the windchime from the wall.

"No, Mimi, it wasn't your fault. It was—"

"Of course it's my fault! It's always my fault." Mimi strode across the room. She opened the cupboard under the sink and slammed the windchime into the bin.

Hemi stepped towards her. "Mimi..."

But she didn't look at him. Her trembles turned to

tears, and she started to sob. She pushed past Hemi and ran upstairs. Coco whimpered, and took a few steps as if to follow her, then came back to Adeline's side, nosing at her hand.

Hemi and Adeline stared at each other. "I really didn't mean to blame her," Adeline said quietly. She swore she wasn't usually this useless at communication. It was like everything went fuzzy when she was around Mimi, all her words dissolving into meaningless noise.

"I know you didn't, babe." He touched her shoulder gently. "I don't know what that was about." He glanced at the feathers on the porch and frowned.

"Go," Adeline told him. "I'll clean this up; you go talk to Mimi."

Hemi let out a breath. "Are you sure?"

Adeline gave a tired smile. "Of course. Besides, this one is desperate to help me." Coco nosed at the feathers, taking advantage of Adeline's distraction.

Hemi smiled and rubbed the Labrador's head. "Okay, but let me know if you need help. Don't go exhausting yourself, yeah?"

Adeline rolled her eyes. "Who me?" Not that it would take much to exhaust Adeline right now. After two days with very little sleep, she felt dead on her feet, but she could still clean up a few feathers.

Hemi kissed her cheek, then headed upstairs. She heard him knock on Mimi's door.

The feathers did look dramatic. She could understand why Mimi had got a fright initially, though her reaction did seem a bit extreme. Perhaps she was afraid of birds? Phobias could be intense, and Adeline didn't want to make her feel worse. Had she been wrong to mention the wind-chime? She really hadn't meant anything by it. The bird getting caught was an accident, and she doubted the chime being there would have made much difference to the outcome, especially as it seemed like the bird had got away safely.

Adeline grabbed the broom from the end of the porch and swept the feathers into a pile. She went back inside to get the dustpan from under the sink, then paused. One of the pipes from the windchime poked out of the top of the bin. Adeline pulled it out, brushing off an old slice of cucumber which had attached itself to the side.

Vibrations hummed through Adeline's hand, sending a tingling charge up her arm and through her body, like an electric shock. She yanked her hand away, dropping the chime on the bench. The sensation travelled through her still, and everything became muffled behind the sound of the hum. Adeline's heart pounded. The sound was the same as the one that echoed in her ears when she was about to pass out. Her head swirled in response.

Adeline stumbled towards the sink as if she could outrun the vibrations. She turned on the tap, letting the water run over her palms. The hum quieted, but Adeline could still feel it, almost as if a thin layer of magic had settled over her, disconnecting her from the world.

This was definitely not caused by the wind; the chime was spelled. No wonder the bird had hit it! Was this why

Mimi felt guilty? Had she tried to use magic, and instead created a powerful object? But if so, what had she been trying to do?

Adeline studied the metal pipes, not wanting to get too close. Mimi was family. She couldn't possibly have been trying to do anything bad, could she? Adeline swallowed. Her own great-great-grandfather, Charles, had technically been family, and he'd done some awful things.

No. Adeline couldn't let herself think that.

Adeline wrapped the chime in a paper towel, not wanting to touch it with her bare skin, then dumped it out in the backyard, closing the door on it. Her anxiety eased as she did. She would deal with it in a moment, but first she needed to get rid of the feathers. She grabbed the dustpan and brush, taking them back out to the porch, a protective intention forming in the back of her mind as she did.

Coco sat beside the pile of feathers, staring at them but not touching.

"Good boy!" Adeline told him.

He wiggled his tail but didn't take his eyes off the pile. Adeline crouched down, ready to scoop it up. An uneasy feeling crept over her again. Something about this didn't look right. Usually, when she'd seen the aftermath of a bird's skirmish, the plumes left behind were all different sizes and shades, often littered with small downy pieces. When there were larger feathers, they'd usually been broken or at the very least a bit battered.

These had a uniform shape and colour, minimal

damage marking them. It was almost as if someone had bought a handful of dyed feathers from a craft shop and scattered them on the doorstep.

Coco nudged Adeline's leg. She looked down at him. "What do you think? Is this someone's attempt at a spell?"

Adeline's stomach dropped. *Mimi's attempt at a spell...?*

No, she didn't want to go there. There had to be another explanation – she just had to find it.

Adeline did another quick search of the porch. She found a chocolate bar wrapper in one corner, and copious amounts of old leaves, but nothing that seemed magical, or gave her any clues as to who might have been out there the night before.

Coco stared up at her, his eyes solemn. Could the ghosts have left the feathers? If so, where would they have got them? She'd seen spirits move objects before, but usually only in short bursts, throwing something across a room. Scattering the feathers would have required not only finding them, but somehow transporting them across the city to her house. Unless they'd manifested them out of the air... but that raised more questions than it answered.

Adeline glanced up the stairs. Mimi's door was firmly shut, Hemi on the other side.

Something niggled at Adeline... something she was supposed to do... The thought circled in the back of her mind, but it just wouldn't form. She sighed, rubbing her temple. Hopefully it would come back to her later if it were important.

Adeline stared down at the dustpan full of feathers. Whatever was happening here, it was beyond Adeline's level of magical understanding.

"What do you think, puppy? Shall we go ask Clara and Lola?"

Coco's tail wags turned into whole bum wiggles at the mention of Adeline's cousin and her guide dog. Adeline just hoped Lola got the message before Clara had to leave for work.

CHAPTER FIVE

wo small children bounded up to Adeline as soon as she entered the park. Adeline's hand tightened on Coco's lead automatically. "Sit, Coco!" He was good with kids, but he did sometimes get a little too enthusiastic, licking their faces or snuffling in their ears.

The little girl held out her hand, letting Coco sniff. The boy just stared at Adeline, in that unnerving way kids do sometimes. He kicked his feet against the gravel path, spraying a shower of small stones into the grass.

"Um... Coco's actually a working dog and..." With adults, that was all Adeline had to say, and they'd realise they weren't supposed to pat right now. The girl looked up at Adeline, frowning. She patted Coco's head, ignoring the bright red "DO NOT TOUCH" embroidered on his coat.

"I've got a dog at home," she told Adeline. The boy was still staring, and Adeline swore he could see into her soul.

"Oh… neato." *Neato?* Where had that come from? She cursed herself for her awkwardness, then slipped Coco's harness over his head, taking him off duty. That solved the problem of the kids patting him at least.

Coco jumped up, his bouncy energy returning now he was in dog-mode. The girl gasped, surprised by his sudden movement. She stepped towards Adeline, slipping her hand into Adeline's.

"Um…" Adeline's voice shot up a few octaves. Was this inappropriate? The girl was clearly just scared, but surely Adeline shouldn't be holding hands with a stranger's kid. "Where are your grownups?" she asked.

"Mum's in the playground," the boy said, speaking for the first time. He pointed, and Adeline turned to see a very pregnant woman waddling towards them.

"Kids, come back over here, please!" she called.

The boy grabbed his sister's hand and pulled her away. Adeline breathed a sigh of relief.

"Bye, doggie!" the little girl called.

Adeline watched until the kids reunited with their mother. She wasn't sure how the woman did it. Keeping track of Coco at the park was hard enough, let alone two wandering kids and a third on the way. Adeline touched her stomach, anxiety filling her at the thought.

Adeline made her way further into the park, passing the reflection pool, and the Katherine Mansfield memorial. A flash of something moving caught Adeline's eye, and then a black Labrador ran towards her. Adeline dropped into a crouch, smooshing the familiar's face as Lola tried to lick hers.

"Yes, hello, Lola. Good girl. Good girl."

The dog wagged her tail, recognising her name. She greeted Coco and the two of them ran off together, going to sit side by side on the sloping lawn as they always did.

Adeline scanned the park, looking for her cousin. Clara sat on a bench at the top of the slope, her back to the motorway. Her red hair stood out against the green of the grass and bushes. Adeline glanced towards the playground, checking the kids were safely back with their mum, then made her way over to her cousin.

"Have a seat," Clara said before Adeline had even reached her.

"Did Lola tell you to meet me here?" Adeline asked.

Clara raised an eyebrow. "She did. But I wasn't sure whether there was something wrong or if she just wanted to see Coco."

Adeline laughed. "A little of both, perhaps?"

With their familiars, it was sometimes hard to tell what was magical intuition, and what was straight Labrador. Occasionally, Adeline followed Coco, thinking he was leading her towards something of great witchy importance, but when they got there, it turned out to be a piece of bread discarded on the pavement, perfect to be snaffled up by a hungry Labrador stomach.

"So, what's up?" Clara asked.

"The usual – ghosts."

Clara's lips quirked into a smirk. "Of course…" Clara hesitated. "Anything else?"

Adeline heard the query in Clara's voice, behind the laughter, and a little pang of guilt shot through her. She still hadn't told Clara about her pregnancy. It was getting more and more obvious that Clara knew and was impatiently waiting for Adeline to tell her. Adeline wasn't sure where her reticence was coming from. It probably had something to do with her health problems. Nothing had ever gone simply for Adeline, so she was expecting her pregnancy to be full of complications as well. Hiding it from everyone wasn't going to change that, but Adeline still wasn't ready to tell anyone.

"Hemi's cousin is staying with us," Adeline said instead. "She's brought several ghosts with her."

Clara frowned. "Ghosts aren't my specialty – you've probably had more experience with them than me by this point – but… that's a little unusual, isn't it?"

"Definitely." Adeline was new to being a witch, but ghosts had always been a part of her life. She'd gotten a sense of what was normal, and what wasn't, and though Hemi had seemed rather blasé about the whole thing, she had a growing feeling of unease about the ghosts following Mimi. Not to mention their behaviour last night, and the strange feathers on the doorstep this morning.

Clara reached out her hand. "Do you want to show me what happened?"

Adeline hesitated. While her cousin's ability to glean information from Adeline's memories was an incredibly useful tool, Adeline hadn't let Clara do it since she became pregnant.

She took a breath. Helping Mimi was more important than her worries about what else Clara might see. Adeline reached out, taking Clara's hand. Clara breathed in matching her inhales to Adeline's, and Adeline let her memories run through her mind, the important details flowing through to Clara.

It was always a strange sensation, but at the same time, Adeline had missed this. Clara was her family, and she loved the closeness that came from being able to share her thoughts in this unique way.

Clara gave her hand a little squeeze, then released it. "The feathers on the doorstep..." she said. "That's very strange."

"I know."

Adeline didn't know what to make of any of it. She'd been hoping Clara would immediately be able to give her answers, but the witchy world very rarely worked that way. Anxiety grew in her stomach. She'd come to rely on her cousin's knowledge of magic to reassure her. It didn't help that these types of situations had become more and more common.

"Did you tell me something about one of Hemi's ancestors seeing ghosts?" Clara asked.

Adeline nodded. "His grandmother, yes."

"Interesting. It could be Mimi has inherited a remnant of that – not the full ability to see them, but some level of awareness. It doesn't explain why the ghost didn't seem to be able to see you, though."

"No. And I'm still not sure whether Mimi can see him either."

Adeline wondered whether Mimi had known about her grandmother's powers. Yet another thing she would need to get Hemi to talk to her about – not so easy when he was working nights. She hoped he'd made some progress this morning.

Hemi was rostered on for a few more late shifts, and then he would have a couple of days off before he switched to morning shifts. Adeline brightened, as she remembered that she had planned leave for his days off so that they could spend some time together. Of course, that was before they knew Mimi was coming to stay, though if Mimi continued spending most of her time hiding in her room, it probably wouldn't make that much difference to their plans.

Now that they had another ghost-chasing adventure to occupy them, their plans may have to change anyway. Adeline chuckled to herself. Most couples took up rock climbing or went to games nights when they needed a shared hobby. Their ghost hunting adventures were certainly unusual, but she had to admit it had made for some fun date nights.

"What time is it?" Clara asked.

Adeline glanced at the time on her phone. "Eight fifteen."

Clara made a noise in her throat. "I've got to get to work, but I'll ask around the witch community – see if anyone has heard of anything like this before."

"Thanks." Adeline stood as her cousin did, and both Coco and Lola came running back to them. They sat in front of their humans, ready to go back into work mode, now they'd had some time to play.

"Are hugs okay today?" Adeline asked. Secretly she really hoped the answer was yes. She needed the hug herself, but she knew she didn't like it when people touched her unexpectedly, and that was even more intense for Clara when she couldn't see it coming.

"Yes, please." Clara reached out and Adeline wrapped her in a hug.

Adeline melted into the embrace for a moment, then pulled back. "You should come over while Mimi's here – have the cousins meet the cousins."

Clara smiled. "I'd like that."

Adeline was the first in the office. She switched on the lights and got herself a glass of water from the kitchen, then got straight to work. Her boss had been really supportive with letting her go home early and adjust hours so that she could take breaks when she needed to. Her morning sickness seemed to be worst in the middle of the day – something to do with the heat, she suspected – so she'd been taking longer lunches to manage it as well. Still, she didn't want to push his kindness by not completing her share of the work.

She heard the office door open. Coco's head lifted from his paws, and he peeked out from under the desk, sniffing the air.

"Hey, Dana," Adeline called.

Dana's laugh rang out. She came around the corner, her warm aura lighting the room. She carried a large Tupperware container, which she rested on Adeline's desk. "Is there an office ghost giving you updates on who comes and goes?"

Adeline flinched at the casual mention of her ability to see ghosts, but Dana winked, and Adeline forced herself to relax. No one else had arrived yet, she reminded herself. Even if the office had been full, no one would have taken Dana's comment literally.

"No, just Coco," she told Dana. "He can smell your treats a mile away."

Coco stretched up, inching his nose towards the container.

Dana grinned. "Clever puppy."

Coco's tail thumped, and Dana reached out a hand as if to pat him. Adeline opened her mouth, but Dana caught herself before Adeline had to say anything.

"Oops, almost forgot, he's on duty. You'd think I'd know by now!"

"I'm the same with Lola." Adeline often had to remind herself to check whether her cousin's guide dog was off duty before patting. She should know better but something about the squishy Labrador faces made all common sense fly out the window.

"You feeling okay today?"

"Yeah, I'm fine." Adeline's words were punctuated with a yawn, which probably took some of the credibility out of them. She laughed. "Or maybe I'm tired. Hemi's cousin's been keeping us up." That wasn't exactly fair to Mimi, but Adeline didn't have the energy to explain the whole story again.

"Is she your first house guest since Hemi moved in?" Dana gave a little laugh. "That'll be a good test for you both."

Adeline frowned. Mimi's presence wouldn't cause problems between her and Hemi, would it? They'd survived a house full of people at Christmas, but she supposed that had only been a couple of nights. Was that why Hemi had been so nervous about Mimi coming to stay?

Dana laughed. "I'm kidding, babe. Here." She opened the Tupperware container, pulling out a cupcake. "Sounds like you need the sugar today."

Adeline had to admit, breakfast felt like a long time ago, and the sweet treat was very welcome. "These are delicious. What's the occasion?"

"Talia's bringing the baby in. She'll be here soon."

Adeline swallowed too soon, the cake hitting the back of her throat. She coughed, and Coco's ears pricked up. He watched her carefully, ready to intervene if she needed help.

"You okay?" Dana slapped Adeline on the back, but Adeline waved her away.

"I'm all right. Just need some water." Adeline sipped from the glass she'd got earlier. Talia left for maternity leave a couple of months ago. Adeline had spent the last few weeks Talia worked with them avoiding her at all costs, sure she would detect Bump with some kind of supersonic baby-dar. Silly, she knew, but pregnant people seemed to have a sixth sense for spotting each other.

The office door opened. "That might be her now." Dana made a beeline for the entrance, and from the amount of cooing that bounced its way over the cubicle walls, there was indeed a baby in the office.

Adeline stood, wrapping her jacket around her waist. "I know *you'll* be excited about babies." She said to Coco.

He wagged his tail, definitely excited about the possibility of small humans and cake crumbs. Talia made her way over to Adeline's desk, and Adeline greeted her with a hug.

"Oh, I've missed you girls!" Talia's aura glowed pink. It mixed with Dana's orange, filling the room with warmth. Adeline felt herself soften. She loved her little workplace family, and it would be lovely for her baby to have a first friend in Talia's son.

"And this is baby Caleb," Talia said.

Dana had captured Caleb and peered down at him adoringly. He did look pretty cute, his little face smooshed against her. Coco inched his way over, and sniffed at the end of Caleb's blanket, his tail waving like mad.

"Don't worry," Talia whispered. "I'm sure we'll be able to pry him away from her eventually."

Dana clucked her tongue. "Oh, all right. Aunty Adeline can have a cuddle." Dana moved towards Adeline.

She definitely knows, Adeline thought. There was no way Dana would give up baby cuddles otherwise. It probably wouldn't be long until the two of them were making comments about Adeline needing practice.

Adeline reached out to take Caleb from Dana but then froze. Her hands trembled, and a queasiness came over her. She stepped back, folding her arms across her body.

"Hey, what's wrong?" Talia asked.

Adeline shook her head. "Probably nothing, I'm just a bit shaky."

"Here." Talia pulled up Adeline's chair. "Eat another one of Dana's cupcakes. That's bound to set you right."

Adeline laughed. "It's probably the sugar that's done it!" She looked to Coco. He was still busy sniffing at Caleb's feet. He hadn't given her any kind of alert, so it didn't seem like she was going to have a seizure or pass out.

Dana reached out again, to give her Caleb now she was sitting, but something in Adeline's chest squeezed at the thought. "Probably not a good idea," she said tightly. She didn't even want to think about what would happen if she fainted while holding him.

Dana frowned, and she saw a glance pass between her and Talia. Then Dana smiled and sat down next to her. "More snuggles for me then." She brought Caleb close, so Adeline could see him.

Adeline's apprehension melted. "Look at his little hands!"

"I know!" Dana practically squealed. "I swear my ovaries skipped a beat when he grabbed my thumb."

"You're going to have trouble getting him back, Talia!"

Adeline could just imagine Dana's delight when there were two babies to snatch away for office cuddles. All Adeline's plans of catching up on work disappeared. She could see the rest of the morning dissolving into baby talk.

"Are you sure you don't want to hold him, Adeline?"

Adeline swallowed. She glanced at Coco. It would be okay – he would let her know if she was going to collapse. "Okay, but you have to take him straight away if Coco gives an alert."

Talia smiled. "It's okay. I trust you."

Adeline looked at Coco again, before taking Caleb from Dana. She felt a surge of hormones as soon as he was in her arms. The weight and warmth of him made her feel all gooey. Coco didn't give any kind of alert. He lay on her feet, his tail waving every so often, as he stretched up to sniff Caleb's feet.

A lump formed in Adeline's throat, and she felt her eyes fill. Dana touched her shoulder, gently.

"Babies will do that to you," Talia said.

Adeline just nodded. There was a long silence after that, and Adeline could tell they were waiting for her to confirm her pregnancy. Instead, Adeline just stared down at Caleb, blinking as her eyes welled.

CHAPTER SIX

Surprisingly, Adeline actually made it through a full day of work, despite the sleep deprivation. On their way out, Coco did a quick tour of the desks, snuffling up cupcake crumbs, much to the delight of their co-workers. Honestly, Adeline had a suspicion that was half the reason Dana brought baking so often.

Adeline barely remembered the walk home. She held tight to Coco's harness and let him take the lead. He pulled her along, giving her the momentum to keep moving. She swore they both breathed a sigh of relief when they made it home. No ghosts greeted them, nor any feathers, bones, or anything else odd – thank goodness for small mercies.

She moved to open the door, then hesitated. Voices came from inside. Perhaps she had spoken too soon when she said there were no ghosts.

"It's happening again," Mimi said, "feathers all over the doorstep!"

"Shh…" came an unfamiliar male voice in response. "It's okay, I'm here."

"It's not! I'm cursed," Mimi said. "It's all going to start happening again."

There it was again – this belief that Mimi was cursed, or that it was her fault these things were happening. Was that what the ghosts were latching onto? Had her guilt somehow made them start following her? Or was it simply a by-product of the chaos they were causing around her?

"It won't, I promise," the man said. "None of that will happen while I'm here."

Adeline hesitated. She didn't want to interrupt, but she couldn't exactly stay on the doorstep listening in either. "Mimi?" she called. "It's just me."

She got no answer, but the voices continued from inside. She let Coco lead her forward into the living room. Mimi stood in the centre of the room, one arm wrapped protectively around herself, the other clutching at her necklace as if it were a lifeline. Beside her stood a man Adeline didn't know – alive, but still unknown. He had an arm around Mimi, gently rubbing her shoulder, but Mimi's face was turned away.

"You're safe now," he said. "I can keep you safe."

Adeline hovered in the doorway. Neither Mimi nor the stranger looked her way. It was an odd feeling to come home and find someone she didn't know in the house.

She'd lived alone for a long time, and even just having Hemi move in had taken some getting used to. She liked the feeling of sharing the space with him, and she was happy to have his family visit, but it felt odd to walk in on such an intense conversation.

"Hi…" Adeline said, finally capturing their attention.

"Oh… I didn't hear you come in." Mimi broke away from the man, an odd look on her face. For a moment, she didn't seem to know what to do with herself, then she moved toward Coco, reaching out to pat him.

"Um…" Adeline hesitated. She already felt on the back foot, and she could see Mimi was going through something, but she also didn't want to encourage Mimi to pat Coco while he was still in work mode. Coco looked up at her, clearly conflicted. He backed away a pace, tucking himself behind Adeline.

Adeline could tell he was focused on the fact that she wasn't feeling well. Her head began to swim, and she leaned against the wall. Mimi frowned. She was still reaching out to pat Coco, but he'd moved away from her.

"Can you not pat him when he's working?" Adeline said.

Mimi's eyebrows shot up, and she stepped back. "Yeah, okay, whatever." She turned away, but Adeline still caught the eye roll.

Adeline swallowed. Every so often someone reacted badly to her asking them not to pat Coco while he was working. She wasn't used to it from family, though. Hemi had explained the rules to Mimi. Adeline understood it was easy to forget, but she wasn't sure it warranted the hostility.

"Just give me a few minutes and I'll take his jacket off. You can have a pat then." Adeline aimed this half towards Mimi's guest, as she felt too awkward to look directly at Mimi right in that moment. Mimi didn't look at her either, and Adeline felt a new level of coldness coming off her.

She had a flashback to being 13, and Hemi's mother introducing her to Mimi. She remembered a similar level of awkwardness then. Mimi had been surly and uninterested in Hemi's little friend.

"I'm Adeline by the way," Adeline said to the man.

Mimi frowned, and Adeline immediately regretted speaking to him, but the man flashed Adeline a smile and held out his hand. "Hadley."

Adeline glanced at Mimi, but Hemi's cousin looked pointedly in the other direction. Adeline took Hadley's hand. A pulse of magic surged through his palm as they shook, vibrating up her arm. Adeline withdrew her hand quickly. Hadley's smile faltered, then his lips stretched, and another pulse flickered out towards her.

Adeline blinked. It was simple charm magic, designed to make people like him, almost indistinguishable from natural charisma. She'd never thought of using magic like that. It didn't seem honest somehow, but she supposed it was no different to mirroring body language or all the other little tricks people used to try and make others react positively toward them. She wasn't even sure if Hadley knew he was doing it.

"Are you staying for dinner?" she asked him. Secretly, she hoped the answer was no. She had no idea if she even had enough food in the cupboard to feed herself, let alone Mimi and her friend.

Hadley glanced at Mimi, but she just shrugged non-committally. "You probably need to get going, right?"

Adeline frowned. Perhaps it would have been better if she'd not come in at that moment. Mimi and Hadley had clearly been in the middle of something – something to do with those feathers.

Hadley flashed Mimi a cheesy smile. "There's never anywhere I'd rather be than with you."

Mimi made a face, not on board with the cheese, and he let out another one of those pulses, trying to win her over. Perhaps this was an in-joke between them. Adeline couldn't quite grasp their relationship. It seemed to shift from moment to moment, maybe in part because of the magic Hadley was using.

Something caught Adeline's eye behind Hadley. A coil of smoke began to swirl, taking shape.

"Not now," Adeline said under her breath.

"Huh?" Mimi glanced at her.

All around the room, faceless ghosts formed. Adeline recoiled. She was used to ghosts, but the faceless spectres surrounding them made her skin crawl.

"Leave us," she whispered. She dropped her handbag as she did, letting the contents spill out over the floor.

"Are you okay?" Mimi moved to help her pick things up.

Adeline nodded. "I'm fine, just dizzy." She stooped to pick up the scattered items, quickly forming a protective intention in her mind.

The ghosts froze in place, but they didn't disappear. Her magic relied on carefully chosen actions paired with powerful intentions and dropping the bag hadn't been the most well-thought-out action. Besides which, she was finding it hard to keep the intention clear in her mind.

It wasn't a lie saying she was dizzy. Adeline's head swum as she straightened up, and Coco pressed against her legs, warning her she was about to pass out. Mimi's arm slipped through hers, guiding her over to the couch.

"Here, let me get you some water." Hadley rushed to the kitchen.

"Hun, maybe you better go if Adeline's not feeling well," Mimi called after him.

"Don't be silly, love," he called back. "I can help. You might need me."

His words sounded odd, but Adeline couldn't put her finger on why. Perhaps it was just the way sound distorted when she was about to faint.

Hadley returned with the water and held the glass out to Adeline. She hesitated. The magic he was using wasn't harmful, but she found herself reluctant to let him close to her regardless. Darkness closed in at the edges of her vision, making the decision for her. She reached for the glass.

A shock of magic, like static electricity, hit her as his fingers brushed against hers, and she drew her hand away quickly. She took a few sips of the water, then nearly spilled it, dizziness taking over.

Mimi took the glass from her, concern scrunching her face. "I don't know what to do. Should I call Hemi?"

"No, don't call him. I'm all right, you don't need to stay," Adeline told Hadley.

"It's okay, I don't mind." Hadley put his arm around Mimi, and she tensed. He rubbed her shoulder, and she relaxed a bit. His little charm spell didn't work on Adeline, but she could practically see it washing over Mimi.

Adeline's head began to clear as her blood pressure stabilised. The ghosts stood frozen in place, not disappearing but not converging on Mimi at least. Perhaps Hadley was keeping her safe in some way, just as he had promised her.

A smoky haze took the place of the darkness at the edge of Adeline's vision. The ghost with the moustache took form in the centre of the room. He stared at Mimi, and slowly moved towards her.

"Don't—" Adeline stood, but the ghost dove forward, hitting the glass of water in Mimi's hands. It flew upwards, smashing into Mimi's lip. Hadley darted back as the water splashed over him. Mimi screamed and clutched her face.

"Oh my god, are you okay?" Adeline rushed to her side.

Mimi pulled her hand away from her face. Red stained her lips like uneven makeup, and her eyes filled with tears.

The ghost took a few steps back. He watched Mimi, a smile on his face. Coco whimpered. He danced on the spot, unsure whether to attend to Adeline or Mimi.

"Go away," Adeline whispered to the ghost, her voice firm.

"Huh?" Mimi mumbled through her hands.

Adeline shook her head. "Nothing."

Adeline wasn't sure if the ghost had heard her, but he disappeared, nonetheless. The others stayed where they were, like silent sentries guarding the room.

Adeline grabbed the first aid kit Hemi had made up for her, pulling out some gauze. She ran it under the tap, cooling it, then pressed it to Mimi's face. Her intention was stronger this time, using the action to create a strong protection around Mimi. The ghosts became agitated as she did, backing away and then disappearing one after the other.

Strangely, Hadley had backed off too. His face had gone pale and sweat beaded on his forehead.

"Just go," Mimi mumbled from behind the gauze. "I'll talk to you tomorrow."

Hadley shook his head. "No... no, I'll be okay."

Mimi rolled her eyes. "He hates the sight of blood," she told Adeline.

Adeline flashed Hadley a sympathetic smile and wiped the trickle of blood from Mimi's chin. "It's fine. I've got her. You go."

Hadley swallowed, his nausea palpable. "Yes... okay, maybe you're right. I'll..." He moved towards Mimi as if to kiss her goodbye, but then seemed to think better of it. He raised his hand into an awkward wave instead, as he backed towards the door. "Feel better, both of you."

Coco followed him out as if to make sure he left, and then came back to lie on Mimi's feet. Mimi visibly relaxed as he did.

"Good boy, Coco." Adeline could feel he was using his familiar magic to help calm and heal Mimi. She joined him, switching her intention from protecting Mimi from the ghosts to helping her heal from the wound.

Mimi took the gauze from her. "It's fine. You should sit down."

As if waiting for that cue, Adeline suddenly felt dizzy again. Coco stood, nudging against her legs, alerting her to her falling blood pressure. She sat down on the couch, and Coco jumped up next to her, laying his head on her lap and staring at her. She stroked his head, calming herself, and letting his magic work on her too. It was funny how her body could do that – holding it together when there was any kind of emergency, but collapsing almost immediately afterwards.

Mimi watched her closely. "You're not going to have a seizure, are you?"

Adeline shook her head, though the movement made the room swim. "No, it's just my blood pressure. It's been all over the place since..." Adeline cut herself off. Now was not the time for baby news. "Hemi didn't mention you had a partner," she said instead.

Mimi scrunched up her nose. "Hadley's not exactly..."

It was Mimi's turn to cut herself off. "I didn't know he was going to come down here."

Adeline kept stroking Coco, pouring soothing magic for all of them into the gesture. "Is he the one who's been texting you? I saw you had a lot of unanswered messages the other day."

Mimi shot her a look, and Adeline immediately regretted the words. If she hadn't been so dizzy, there's no way she would have said that.

"You were looking at my phone?"

"No, no, I just saw the screen when you picked it up. But you're right, I shouldn't have been looking. I'm sorry."

"You're damn right, you shouldn't have been."

Mimi spat the words out, and Adeline blinked at her. She knew she was in the wrong, but did it really warrant that much anger?

"I'm sorry. I just meant…" What did Adeline mean? She wasn't exactly sure herself. From the conversation she'd overheard, it sounded like Hadley was comforting Mimi, being exactly the support Mimi needed in the face of her supposed curse. But Adeline couldn't shake the feeling that something was wrong. Perhaps it was the magic Hadley used, or perhaps Adeline was just getting confused, mistaking the energy she felt from the ghosts for him.

She shook her head. She tried to get up, but Coco put his paw over her lap, keeping her in place. "I just meant if there's an issue, maybe Hemi and I could—"

"There's not." Mimi glared at her, and Adeline found

herself shrinking under the gaze. The silence hung for a moment, then Mimi sniffed. "I'm going out for a bit."

Adeline wanted to ask whether that was a good idea when Mimi's face was literally bleeding, but she bit her tongue, keeping the comments to herself. From Mimi's point of view, she'd just slipped, hitting herself in the face with the glass. She hadn't seen the ghost, or how happy he'd seemed at having injured her.

"We'll see you later then, I guess."

Mimi hovered for a moment as if there was something else she wanted to say, then she turned and stomped out, without looking back.

Adeline sighed. "I made a mess of that, didn't I, puppy?"

Coco wagged his tail, unfortunately agreeing with her.

CHAPTER SEVEN

$\mathcal{A}$deline stared into the cupboards, wondering what to make for dinner. She wasn't hungry, but if she wanted to make amends with Mimi, food was probably going to be her best bet. But, with everything else that had been happening, grocery shopping hadn't been high on her priority list, and the cupboards were looking decidedly empty. The fridge was slightly better, though she didn't really think offering limp salad leaves and wrinkly tomatoes would do her any favours. Worst of all, she was out of coffee. She wouldn't get anywhere with Mimi, or Hemi for that matter, if she deprived them of caffeine.

"What do you think?" she said to Coco. "Shall we head to the supermarket and get some supplies?"

Coco wagged his tail. She wasn't sure if he understood what she was saying but he was always a fan of going to the supermarket, mainly because he often found the odd stray nut or loose oat in the pick and mix aisle. Adeline slipped his harness on, and they set off.

Adeline had only intended to do a quick shop, enough to make dinner and restock basic supplies, but she found herself strolling the aisles loading up the trolley. A part of her knew it was about avoiding going back home. Even though Mimi had gone out, Adeline knew she'd end up sitting around waiting for her to come home. Strange how one person could completely change the dynamic of a household. The bright lights and colourful packaging were just the distraction Adeline needed. There was no mental space left to think about anything else in such an excessively high stimulus environment.

Adeline turned into the bread aisle, and a familiar wispy figure greeted her. "Hey, Stanley," she called.

The ghost continued his pacing as he always did. Adeline noticed his lips were moving, but he didn't seem to be saying anything.

"It's me, Adeline," she said.

Stanley was one of the more confused ghosts Adeline had encountered, and he couldn't always remember who she was. He couldn't always remember who *he* was, for that matter. Sometimes he seemed to forget he was a ghost.

"Are you okay, Stanley?"

He didn't answer. He continued his pacing, walking towards her until he passed right through her body. Adeline shivered. It wasn't like there was any real reaction to it; she couldn't feel anything, as the spirit slipped through her. It was just the strangeness of it. Now she was closer, she could see that he was still speaking, but she couldn't hear the words.

"You can't see me, can you?" Adeline leaned back against the wall doing her best not to knock the shelves of bread. Something heavy seemed to be growing inside her chest. She swallowed, desperately trying not to cry in the supermarket. The ghosts Mimi had brought with her couldn't see her, and she couldn't hear them. She couldn't even see their faces. Now Stanley couldn't hear her either.

Adeline's heart sank. Yesterday, Katherine Mansfield had ignored her... or had she? Maybe Katherine couldn't see her anymore either.

Coco looked up at her, his little face worried.

"It's okay, puppy," she told him. "Mum's just sad."

Coco wagged his tail, recognising that she was talking to him, but not understanding her words. That seemed to be a pattern at the moment. Adeline couldn't help herself and started to cry in earnest.

"Hey, chicky."

Adeline looked up at the voice. Dana stood in front of her. Her head tipped to the side in sympathetic concern. Somehow that just made Adeline cry more.

"Aw, sweetheart." Dana wrapped her arms around

Adeline, and Adeline leaned her head on her colleague's shoulder. "What is it? What's wrong?"

"Everything." Adeline knew it was dramatic, but right now it really did feel that way.

Behind Dana, Stanley continued his pacing taking absolutely no notice of either of them.

Dana walked home with Adeline. They passed Kate Sheppard and Katherine Mansfield. Both spirits ignored them, simply floating along the street, as they had in the past before the ghosts started talking to Adeline. Her eyes welled up again at that. She was losing her connection to the ghosts.

Adeline wondered if this was simply things returning to the status quo, now that whatever her great-great-grandfather had done had been put to right. Somehow the thought felt heavy in her chest.

"I'm sorry," Adeline said. "I don't know what that was. I just got overwhelmed."

Dana chuckled. "Happens to the best of us. We've all cried in the supermarket at least once." Dana hesitated, and Adeline could see something spark in her aura. "You're sure there's nothing else going on, though?"

Adeline couldn't look at her. Maybe it was her fault the ghosts couldn't talk to her anymore. She'd spent so much time lately avoiding talking honestly, perhaps it was catching up with her. Still, she shook her head. "There's just some stuff going on with the ghosts… And with Hemi's cousin."

Dana nodded, but she gave a little mouth shrug, and the orange of her aura dimmed a shade. "You know… if there is something else going on, we'll all be supportive."

Adeline looked away. Dana had been nothing but kind to her, and she didn't like disappointing her. "There's not."

Dana sighed. "Yeah, but—"

"I said there's not!" Sudden heat rose inside Adeline, and the words burst out of her. "Why can't you just leave it alone?"

Dana stepped back, startled, and the heat rushed out of Adeline just as quickly as it had come.

"I'm so sorry. That was rude, I just…" Adeline's voice petered out, no explanation coming to her. Or at least, not one she was ready to give.

Dana sniffed, then forced herself to smile. "It's okay. I just meant we'll all be here if you need us."

The offer was still genuine, Adeline could tell, but there was a hesitancy in Dana's voice now, that hadn't been there before.

"Thank you," Adeline said, and she really meant it. "I appreciate you looking out for me."

They stopped outside Adeline's place. Thankfully, there were still no ghosts on the doorstep, and no feathers either. Adeline was particularly glad about that last part. She had almost expected to come home to find another collection waiting for her.

She turned to Dana. "And thank you for walking me home."

Dana flapped her hand, waving the words away. "Of course. It's no big deal."

"No really." Adeline reached out, touching Dana's hand. "It means a lot to me. I'm lucky to have a friend like you."

Dana's aura brightened at that, and she gave Adeline a hug. "I'm always here, chicky. Call me if you need anything."

Adeline watched Dana walk away, the familiar bounce in her colleague's steps returning. She hated the distance keeping secrets was creating. Maybe she just needed to get past this and tell everyone. The thought of it made her chest squeeze tight though, and she knew she'd never find enough air to make the words come out.

She closed her eyes in a slow, stress-releasing blink, then turned to go inside. A rustling around the side of the house made her freeze. Coco's ears pricked up, having heard it too.

Adeline hesitated. If Hemi were here, he would have been begging Adeline to leave it alone, to call him or the police and just let them deal with it. Not that the police would have done much good if it were ghosts. Instead, Adeline made her way to the corner of the house, peering down the gap between the wall and the fence.

A face peered back at her. She stepped back with a gasp. Coco growled, and Adeline heard a curse then a familiar pulse of magic hit her.

"Hadley!"

Hadley hesitated, then stepped forward, coming out into the light. He looked taken aback to find her there, which was ironic given that was her house. What on earth was he doing creeping around outside?

He laughed, then flashed Adeline his trademark charming smile. "Sorry, I didn't mean to startle you."

"Then you shouldn't be lurking around outside my house!"

Hadley chuckled. "True. You caught me. I rang the doorbell, but Mimi didn't answer. I thought she might be out the back."

Adeline nearly pointed out that perhaps Mimi not answering meant she didn't want to see him. Hadley seemed to sense her unspoken words.

"She said she was sunbathing out there the other day," he said sheepishly. "I thought she might not hear me knocking."

Adeline glanced at the sky, dusk sending shadows creeping across it. It had been sunny earlier, though, she had to admit. The back garden wasn't exactly the best place to sunbathe, but she could see the deck working if one were determined.

"Mimi went out," she told Hadley. "I don't know when she'll be back."

"That's okay. I can wait."

Adeline hesitated, then made her way back towards the porch. Coco sniffed Hadley, neither seeming to welcome him nor to give a warning. Hadley followed her around the corner and up the stairs to the house. Adeline wasn't exactly sure she wanted to let him in. Mimi opened the door before Adeline could unlock it.

Adeline stared at her, startled. "I didn't realise you were home." Dammit, now it looked like she had lied to Hadley.

"Just got in." Mimi looked from Adeline to Hadley and her gaze narrowed. She gave an irritated tug on her necklace, freeing a trapped lock of hair. Her lip had stopped bleeding, but a purply bruise marked her skin in its place.

Adeline tilted her head towards Hadley. "I found this one lurking outside." Adeline's tone matched Mimi's annoyed expression.

Mimi's frown deepened. "I told you I was busy this evening, Hadley."

"Not too busy for me, surely." He flashed her a smile. "I just wanted to check on you – make sure your lip is okay. I brought you some chocolate." He held out a block of dark salted caramel.

Mimi hesitated, then reluctantly took it. "Thanks," she mumbled.

Adeline frowned. She really didn't like the way Hadley seemed to dismiss Mimi. If Mimi had said she was busy, he should have respected that. But Mimi seemed to be softening. Something crackled in the air – maybe Hadley's magic – and suddenly faceless ghosts were appearing around Mimi again.

"Mimi, come here quickly!" Adeline reached out a hand, but Mimi frowned at her.

"What? Why?"

Adeline didn't have an answer, but she knew she had to get Mimi away from the ghosts. She rushed into the house, causing Mimi to step back and the ghosts to scatter. Adeline scanned the room looking for them. Little wisps appeared around the room, but none of them took shape.

Suddenly Mimi's hand was on Adeline's shoulder. "Are you okay? Are you having a seizure?"

Adeline glanced back through the door at Hadley. He didn't realise she was looking at him, and he'd dropped the charming smile. His expression twisted into something nasty, full of arrogance and bitterness. He looked up meeting her eye and schooled his face into a look of concern. Adeline could see straight through it.

"No," Adeline said. "Not a seizure, but..." Adeline didn't want to lie, but she really didn't want Mimi leaving the house with Hadley either.

"Come in here," Mimi said, leading Adeline into the living room. "I'll make you a cup of tea."

Hadley stepped into the hallway and the ghosts reappeared again swarming around him. Was he controlling them? Adeline watched, but he didn't seem to be aware of them. They swirled about him, not quite fully forming, but creating a misty haze around him.

"Hey, Hadley, it's really not a good time. I should stay with Adeline."

There was a false note to Mimi's voice. Adeline could tell she was glad of the excuse to tell him to go. Adeline rubbed her head, hoping it made for a convincing perfor-mance. She was sick so often; she never really had the opportunity to fake it. In fact, the idea of doing so made her very uncomfortable, but needs must.

Hadley grimaced. He glanced towards Adeline, and his gaze hardened. She had a sense he knew exactly what was going on, but at least this way, his anger was directed at Adeline, and not Mimi.

He gave a forced smile. "Of course, love. We'll talk later."

He gave Mimi a quick kiss on the cheek which made Mimi tense up, and then he turned and left. An uneasy feeling crept over Adeline. That was simpler than it should have been.

Mimi disappeared into the kitchen, returning a few minutes later with a cup of tea – chamomile from the smell of it. Coco hopped up on the couch, leaning his head against Adeline's lap.

"Are you okay?" Mimi asked. She touched Adeline's hand, and the concern was genuine.

Adeline nodded. "Are you?"

Mimi blinked at the question. For a moment, it seemed like she was going to brush Adeline off, but then she soft-ened. "Yeah, he just doesn't listen when I say I don't want to do something."

"That's not a good sign."

Mimi shrugged. "I guess." It seemed like she wanted to say more, but instead, she just let the silence hang. She picked up Hadley's gift. "Do you want this? I don't really like caramel."

"Mimi…" There were so many things Adeline needed to say, but somehow none of them wanted to come out. Adeline had told Hemi she'd wait for him to talk to Mimi, but that wasn't getting them anywhere. She took a breath and just went for it. "Mimi, I'm sorry about before," she blurted out. "I really don't mean to invade your space, it's just Hemi told me you think you're cursed!"

Mimi's eyes shot up to meet Adeline's. "Jesus, that boy can't keep things to himself, can he?" Mimi stood, her whole body seeming to bristle. Adeline cursed herself for the bluntness of her words. For a moment, it had seemed like they were getting somewhere, but Mimi's whole mind and body were closing off in front of her.

"It's just Hadley…"

"It's none of your business, Adeline. You've got to stop. Just because you're dating Hemi doesn't mean you can pry into my life." Mimi spat the words at her, and Adeline found herself shrinking. Not least because there was something so dismissive about the way Mimi described her as "dating" Hemi as if her place in his life was only temporary as if they weren't having a baby together. But of course. Mimi didn't know about the baby.

Mimi shook her head, refusing to look at Adeline. "Enjoy your tea." She stormed her way upstairs, once again shutting herself in her bedroom.

CHAPTER EIGHT

deline made dinner, calming herself in the process of creating a meal. If her mind had been clearer, she could have used magic, pouring an intention for a peaceful household into the making of the food. As it was, the best she could hope for was an hour's distraction.

The front door opened. Coco leapt up, paws clattering across the floorboards, then Hemi's voice rang out, greeting him.

"Hello, puppy. Aren't you a good boy? Aren't you a good boy?"

Adeline smiled, warmth filling her at having Hemi home. He came into the kitchen, Coco dancing along beside him, excited not only because his human was home, but because his human was home and had brought food. Hemi set a couple of bags of groceries down on the bench.

"Hey." Adeline greeted him with a kiss. "What are you doing here?"

"Quiet night. My boss said I could take a long dinner break." Hemi wrapped his arms around her, nuzzling into her neck. "I thought I could surprise you with dinner… but looks like you've beaten me to it." He gestured to the bags of shopping Adeline had bought earlier which she hadn't yet unpacked. "Great minds, eh?"

"Yeah."

It wasn't the best planning on their part, but with Hemi's appetite and Coco's soulful looks anytime dinner was mentioned, she was sure they'd be able to make their way through the food.

"Do you need any help?"

Adeline shook her head. "Nearly done, but you could put those away if you like?"

Hemi picked up the grocery bags, as she finished preparing the meal. Normally, she preferred to put things away herself, knowing he would place things way too high for her to reach, but she also knew there was no way he'd sit idly by while she did all the work. Besides, on some level she liked having to stretch up to reach things. It reminded her of him at the times when he wasn't around.

Already she felt calmer, just knowing he was home. She'd lived on her own for years, but since Hemi had moved in, she felt unsettled every time he had a prolonged period of night shifts. A part of her felt uneasy about that as if she was losing her independence. But a bigger part of her just loved knowing she had family.

"Is Mimi home?" he asked.

"In her room." Adeline wasn't sure whether to mention her latest run in with Mimi. Every interaction she'd had with Hemi's cousin had been fraught, but somehow this one felt worse. Hemi frowned and Adeline could tell he'd read half of what she was thinking on her face.

"What is it?" he asked. "Did you two fight again?"

Adeline blinked. She wasn't sure she'd describe what they'd been doing as fighting, but it certainly wasn't altogether amicable either. "I don't think she's a fan of me."

Hemi bared his teeth in something which could have been a laugh or a grimace. "You've certainly made an impression."

Well, that wasn't comforting. Adeline rubbed her head pressing the heels of her palms into her eyes. She was just so tired.

Hemi chuckled. "Don't worry about it, babe. Mimi tends to be an acquired taste."

But Adeline did worry, and not just about whether Mimi liked her. She couldn't shake the feeling that something wasn't right with Hadley. The ghosts had gone out of their way to scare Mimi, not to mention hitting her in the face with the glass. If Hadley was somehow controlling them…

"I did tell you to leave it to me."

Adeline looked up at Hemi. His words held a challenge. True, he had told her he would talk to Mimi… but then he hadn't.

"I was going to, but you weren't here." Adeline's voice

came out harsher than she meant it to. She realised she was frustrated with Hemi's casual attitude to what was happening.

He frowned. "I've been on night shifts." His voice came out harsh as well.

Adeline turned back to the food, stirring the pan. She could feel Hemi's eyes on her, then he turned away too, opening a cupboard to put things away.

"Have you managed to talk to the ghosts?" he asked. His voice still held a little irritation and she felt herself shrinking. Being able to talk to ghosts was normally the one useful thing she could offer in situations like this. Right now, that was failing her.

"No," she said. "They won't say anything."

"That's weird, isn't it? Normally ghosts are clamouring for your attention." Hemi punctuated that with a slam of the cupboard door, and Adeline jumped at the noise.

"There's something funny with the ghosts. I can't quite…"

Coco pawed at the back door, and Adeline took the opportunity to trail off. She couldn't articulate what she was feeling. There was something odd about the ghosts and with Hadley, and with Mimi in general. It wouldn't quite come together in her mind, especially with Hemi snarking at her.

She opened the door, letting Coco out into the back garden. "And the ghosts aren't clamouring for my attention." Adeline's tone took on an edge. "None of them are even talking to me."

Hemi frowned. "What do you mean?"

Adeline shrugged. "Kate Sheppard, Katherine Mansfield, even Stanley at the supermarket. None of them seem to be able to see me anymore."

Suddenly, all the attitude went out of her, and sadness welled up inside her. It wasn't like the conversations she had with the ghosts had ever been that meaningful. The ones with her relatives had been, but they've been gone for a while. It just felt odd that she could still see the ghosts, but they couldn't see her. Every time she'd gone to the supermarket she had chatted with Stanley. He'd always been confused, but she'd been able to offer him a few reassuring words, remind him what had happened. Now, he was back to being stuck in that pacing loop. All of them had reverted to their loops whether or not they were happy in them. The thought made her stomach clench.

"I'm sorry." Hemi touched her back, gently, but he didn't hug her. He didn't get it – he couldn't.

His phone beeped, and he picked it up, looking at the screen briefly before frowning and setting it down.

"Is that your mum?"

Hemi looked up at her, surprised. "Yeah."

"Did you call her back?"

Hemi's frown deepened.

"I mean… she's called a couple times now and…" Adeline had the sinking feeling that she'd stepped over a line again, just like she had with Mimi. It seemed to be all she did at the moment with Mimi and with Dana and now with Hemi.

Hemi stared at her for a second then looked away. "I'll call her later." His voice wasn't exactly harsh, but it was closed off.

Adeline turned away again, biting her lip. She didn't want this to turn into a whole thing. She didn't want to cry. *I guess I can always blame it on hormones,* she thought. Though only with Hemi.

"Maybe it's not such a bad thing that you can't hear the ghosts anymore," Hemi said quietly.

Even though she had meant to keep her back turned – to keep her welling eyes turned away – she found her gaze shooting to Hemi.

"What do you mean?"

Hemi sighed. "I don't know… it's just… the ghosts seem to cause a lot of trouble, you know?"

"I guess." It was true that there had been a lot of chaos surrounding the ghosts, but that wasn't exactly their fault. They had been a part of Adeline's life for so long; they were significant to who she was. How could Hemi talk about that disappearing so casually?

"I mean it's not like they've ever bought anything good into your life, right?"

Adeline blinked. Without the ghosts, would she have reconnected with Hemi? Would she have met Clara? Without the ghosts, she wouldn't have found out she was a witch, but perhaps Hemi meant he wished that part of her was gone too.

When she didn't speak, Hemi continued. "I mean, don't you ever wish things could be more normal?"

"You mean you wish *I* could be more normal."

Hemi's eyes widened. "No, I didn't say that."

"I told you I was a witch before we started dating. You were the first person I told."

"That's not what I meant. I love you. I just—"

"Wish I was more normal."

Hemi's expression was changing from worried to angry. "That's not what I said! You know I don't think that."

With everything – the ghosts, her epilepsy, Adeline bringing her dog everywhere they went, and yes, even her being a witch, Hemi had been by her side, accepting through all of it. But maybe he was harbouring some level of resentment – some desire that she could just be *normal*.

There was a thump as Coco came in the back door. Adeline turned to look at him, glad of the distraction. He gave a hissing retch, which usually meant he was about to throw up.

"Coco?" She dashed towards him. His paws clattered on the kitchen tiles. He clawed at his face, scratching his cheek.

"Oh my god, he's choking."

"Shit!" Hemi tried to grab Coco, but he dodged away, too panicked to realise Hemi was trying to help.

Adeline got hold of him and tried to pull his jaws apart, but Coco wrenched away from her, still trying to claw whatever was stuck in his throat out himself.

"Mimi!" Hemi yelled. "Get down here. We need help."

Adeline heard the thump of Mimi making her way

downstairs and swore she could hear resentment in the steps. Mimi appeared in the doorway, her expression morphing as she took in the scene. Hemi managed to get hold of Coco but couldn't get his mouth open.

"He's choking," Adeline said. She felt like she was choking herself; she could barely force the words out.

Mimi's manner turned serious. "What do I do?"

"Call the vet," Adeline told her. "The number's on the fridge."

Mimi grabbed the fridge magnet from the vet and dashed back into the other room to get her phone. Hemi looked up at Adeline. "Babe, you need to use magic."

Coco had gone limp in Hemi's arms. She knew Hemi was right but drawing her power to her right now felt impossible. "An intention and an action," she whispered to herself, her voice breaking.

Right now, the best action would be the obvious, practical one. She knelt down on the floor, prying Coco's mouth apart. He was still conscious, but he let her, his eyes looking up at her, suddenly calm. She reached into his mouth, ignoring the sharp teeth which threatened to clamp down on her wrist. She drew all her magic around her, pouring it into Coco.

Her hand closed on something solid in the back of his throat, and she pulled it free. The whole room crackled with the magic coming from both her and Coco. Adeline opened her hand, revealing a chicken bone. "What the...?"

Mimi came back into the kitchen, the phone to her ear.

"I don't know. He's choking on something." She looked down at Adeline, her eyes falling on the bone in Adeline's hand. "A chicken bone," Mimi whispered. All the colour drained from her face.

Hemi reached up to take the phone from her. "It's okay, we've got it out, but he was choking for a long time. He went limp." Hemi listened for a moment and then nodded as if the vet could see him. "We'll bring him in now… Okay, thank you." He hung up the phone.

Adeline lay down on the floor, wrapping her arms around Coco. She felt his tail wag, tapping against her knee, and she'd never been more grateful for the sensation.

"Where did he get it?" Mimi asked.

Adeline looked up. "What?"

"The bone. Where did he get it? Neither of you eat chicken."

Adeline shrugged. "I don't know. He found one on the doorstep the other day." Right now, she didn't care. She just wanted Coco to be okay.

Mimi suddenly strode across the room, pulling open the back door. She stared out into the garden, her whole body going still, and then she screamed. Coco leapt up, near-death experience forgotten in light of one of his humans being in danger.

"What is it?" Hemi leapt up too, running to join Mimi on the back doorstep. He froze, staring out. "Oh my god."

"What is it?" Adeline asked, repeating Hemi's question.

Hemi turned back to look at her, his face spooked. "They're all over the lawn."

"What are?"

"Bones," Mimi said. "It's happening again."

CHAPTER NINE

*M*imi came with them to the vet. Her face had turned a waxy pale colour, and her hands trembled almost as much as Adeline's. Hemi tried to ask her what she meant by "it's happening again" but she just shook her head. If possible, she went even paler.

Adeline could only focus on Coco.

Hemi wrapped his arm around her. "He's going to be okay."

Adeline nodded. Yes, he would be okay. She was pouring all of her magic into making sure of that.

The vet called her name. Adeline got up, but Coco cowered, still afraid of the vet despite being both an assistance dog and familiar.

"A bit shy, is he?" The vet produced some treats, and Coco perked up, allowing Adeline to lead him into the exam room. The vet checked Coco over, as Adeline explained what had happened.

"Chicken bones on the lawn, huh? Did you have a barbecue or something?"

Adeline shook her head. "No. I don't even eat meat."

"Someone chuck them over the fence? People can be so careless with their rubbish."

Adeline doubted that was what had happened. The bones had been arranged carefully on the lawn. Coco had disrupted some of them, but it was obvious they had started out as a star – a pentacle. Above it, hanging from the side of the shed was the discarded windchime. Adeline couldn't get the image of the bones out of her mind. Someone – or something – had done this deliberately.

"His throat's a bit raw, but he doesn't seem to have done any damage. Keep him quiet this evening, just in case, and perhaps don't let him out in the yard until you're sure you've got rid of all the bones."

Adeline nodded. She would be scouring every inch of the backyard to make sure they had gotten rid of everything before she felt safe to let Coco out there. Even then, it would be a long time before she'd let him be outside alone. If someone had been back there, what else could they have done? Was it just the bones, or were there other dangers waiting to be discovered?

She couldn't believe she'd just forgotten about the windchime. She'd meant to get rid of it, but the thought had disappeared from her mind as soon as it was out of sight – almost as if it had been spelled to be overlooked. The more concerning question was what else was it spelled to do? She had a feeling it was responsible for more than just making noise. Had it been making her forget other things too?

The vet gave Coco a treat, and he gave a little tail wag, still apprehensive about the unusual smells in the exam room. "Feel free to come back in, if you're worried about anything, but I think he'll be fine."

"Thank you so much." Adeline felt her eyes well up again, and Coco licked her face, just happy to be going home.

Coco was much more energetic on his way out of the office, practically running towards Hemi and Mimi. The look of relief that flooded Mimi's face made a pit form in Adeline's stomach. Mimi really seemed to think that it was her fault.

Hemi crouched down, rubbing Coco's neck. "Who's a good boy?" He looked up at Adeline. "All okay?"

Adeline nodded. "Yeah, he's going to be fine."

Hemi smooshed Coco's face, which sent Coco's tail into double time wagging, then Hemi tilted his head towards the door. "Come on. Let's go home."

They made their way back to the car, but Mimi dawdled behind them, checking her phone. Adeline glanced back at her. Mimi rocked on the balls of her feet, the phone held in front of her, but her eyes staring into the middle distance.

"Are you okay?" Adeline asked. She hated that her voice sounded stiff. It wasn't that she blamed Mimi, but she couldn't help but get protective over anything that threatened Coco's safety.

Mimi looked back at Adeline and her expression was so lost. Adeline took a step towards her, any resentment she'd felt a moment ago disappearing. Mimi met her eye and she just seemed so worn down. Then she shook her head. "I'm not coming back with you."

Adeline frowned. "What do you mean?"

Mimi glanced down at her phone then looked away again quickly. "I'm going to go see Hadley."

Hadley. He had been around the side of the house this afternoon; there was no way that was a coincidence. Adeline felt heat rise inside her for the second time that day. She wanted to yell, call Hadley all sorts of names, and tell Mimi she should run as fast as she could in the other direction.

"Don't," was all that came out.

Hemi looked up at her, and Adeline opened her mouth to pour out the whole story. Instead, she found herself crying, tears choking up her throat. Coco whimpered. He pulled toward Mimi, trying to draw his pack together.

"I'm sorry." Mimi backed away from Coco as if afraid to touch him. She didn't meet Adeline's eyes. It was very obvious that meeting Hadley was the last thing she wanted to do, but still, she was walking away from them.

"Don't go, Mimi," Adeline said, but Mimi still turned away, leaving Coco whimpering after her.

Adeline wrapped Coco up in his blanket on the couch. He wagged his tail, pleased with the attention, vet visit already forgotten. The risotto Adeline had been making was cold and congealed on the stovetop but thank goodness Hemi had remembered to turn it off. The last thing they needed was a fire.

"It'll be okay when it's heated up," Hemi said.

Adeline nodded. "Don't you have to get back to work, though? I can make you a sandwich or something to take with you."

He was perfectly capable of making his own sandwich, of course, but that wasn't the point. They'd argued, and sometimes rushing someone out the door with food was easier than talking about it.

Hemi frowned. "Don't you want me to stay? You've had a big fright."

Adeline shook her head. "I'm okay. I'm going to call Clara." She had a feeling her cousin might have some insights into what was going on. The vet was right, Coco was fine, but that didn't change the fact that something very strange had happened tonight… Strange, but maybe not supernatural. Adeline was still trying to figure out exactly what Hadley was up to.

"Besides, there's a better chance Coco will stay settled if it's just me and him. He always wants to play with you."

Coco's ears pricked up, hearing the word "play", and Adeline gave a half-laugh. "See?"

"True." Hemi smiled at Coco, then turned back to Adeline. He stepped towards her but stopped just short of touching her. "I'll help clean up the bones. Leave them until I get back, okay?"

Adeline nodded. As much as she wanted to rush out there right now, she wasn't going to do a very effective clean up in the dark.

Hemi reached out, placing one hand on her arm. "I love you, Adey." He said the words seriously, pouring more meaning into them than three words alone could hold. If he'd been a witch, she was sure she would have felt a loving intention wrapping all the way around her right now, washing away all the things he hadn't meant to say earlier.

"I love you too."

The phone rang only once before Clara picked up. "Adeline?"

Adeline chuckled. "Even over the phone, you know it's me?"

"They don't call me a witch for nothing."

Adeline could hear the smirk in Clara's voice.

"What's happened?" Clara asked. "Lola's been agitated all evening."

Of course. Clara's familiar would have picked up on what was happening to Coco, though explaining it all was beyond even a magical dog's power. "We've been at the vet," she told Clara.

"Coco okay?"

"He nearly choked on a chicken bone. Our yard was covered in them. Laid out like a… like a pentacle." Adeline wished she was in the same room as Clara where she could just transfer her memories to her cousin. She almost wanted to invite Clara to come over now, but there would be no rest with Coco and Lola in the same room together.

"A pentacle?" The quality of the silence in the pause after that told Adeline that this was serious.

"Yes, I think so." To be fair, Adeline hadn't seen a pentacle since she was thirteen, and all the girls in her year went through a "witchy" phase. None of that had been actual magic though, just teenagers experimenting with something that made them feel powerful.

"It was some type of star-circle thing at least," she added. "The guy she's been seeing – Hadley – I caught him around the side of the house this afternoon."

Clara made a noise in her throat. "That can't be a coincidence… And she keeps saying she's cursed, right? Do you think he's gaslighting her?"

"Yes." Adeline let out a breath. Gaslighting was the perfect word for it. Hadley was clearly trying to make Mimi think she was cursed, but *why* exactly? What possible gain could he get from scaring her? "But the thing is, he does have some sort of magic. I felt it when he tried to use it on me. And even if he put the bones on the lawn and the feathers on the doorstep, it doesn't explain the ghosts. Do you think he could be controlling them?"

"I really don't know, Adeline, but this is concerning."

Adeline agreed. Hadley's simple charm magic was probably more dangerous than Adeline had realised. She suspected she had been very lucky it hadn't worked on her.

Adeline stopped short. She hadn't felt like the magic had influenced her, but maybe she was wrong about that. She'd found Hadley sneaking around the side of her house, and not even mentioned it to Hemi. It had taken her far longer than it should have to make the connection between him being there, and the bones lying on the lawn, and yet she *still* didn't tell Hemi. She'd completely forgotten about the windchime, despite the obvious magic coming off it, and she'd made only a weak attempt at stopping Mimi from going to meet Hadley, feeling like she couldn't get the words out, when really, she should have been pulling out all stops to make sure Mimi didn't go off with this dangerous man.

"Clara…" Adeline tried to keep her voice steady. "I think maybe Hadley used some magic on me."

Adeline heard a sharp intake of breath from her cousin, then the sound of Clara's hand tapping against the table. She felt a wave of something calming wash over her. Her cousin was using the rhythm to send her magic down the phone.

"Are there ghosts around you now?" Clara asked.

"No, they only seem to come when Mimi is around, and she's out."

"That's good. You and Coco need to rest right now. Say it with me."

"Coco and I need to rest now." Adeline poured her own magical intention into the words. Adeline's mind was still whirring, all the unanswered questions circling, clamouring for her attention. But the calming magic was stronger, slowing and soothing her troubled thoughts.

"You're right," she found herself saying. "Rest first, magical mystery solving tomorrow."

CHAPTER TEN

Adeline kept her promise, leaving the bones for Hemi to clean up, but she couldn't leave the windchime. She took it down, then thoroughly doused it with the hose. She kept a cleansing intention clear in her mind, letting Hadley's magic run off with the water. Even then, she didn't feel safe with it in the house. She dropped it in the rubbish bin at the kerb, glad the truck would be coming the next morning.

She and Coco spent the rest of the evening cuddled up on the couch, Adeline eating far more of the salted caramel chocolate than she really meant to. At least that wasn't spelled. If it had been, Hadley might have got a flavour Mimi actually liked.

Mimi returned home later that night. Three faceless ghosts floated in the door behind her, and Adeline caught sight of another three lurking on the doorstep.

"I'm just here to get changed," Mimi told her. "I'm heading back out in a minute."

Adeline nodded, unsure what else to say. Mimi hovered for a moment. She trailed her hand along the keys of the old piano in the corner. Discordant notes shuddered under her fingers, not having been played – or tuned – since Adeline was a child. It clunked as Mimi depressed the keys, echoing the mood in the room.

Finally, Mimi headed upstairs, leaving the ghosts to congregate in the living room. Coco seemed uneasy about them, his ears pricked back, and his eyes followed them every time they moved.

Adeline tried to engage with the spirits. They didn't acknowledge her, though perhaps they couldn't without eyes or lips. One of them floated towards the piano, pressing down the same keys Mimi had, in a jarring chord. Adeline closed the piano lid, dampening the unpleasant sound.

When she got nowhere talking to the ghosts, Adeline found shooing them towards the door seemed to work. They behaved as if they couldn't see her, but when she moved towards them flapping her hands as if they were flies, they dodged away and eventually drifted through the front door to hang out with the ones on the doorstep.

Adeline didn't feel good about doing that. She'd spent much of her time, over the last year or so, trying to engage with ghosts and figure out what it was they needed. To be so callous as to shoo them away felt very unnatural, but it was getting unsettling with so many faceless figures lurking around her. She reminded herself that they didn't feel the cold. Standing on the doorstep or on the pavement outside her house wouldn't feel any different to them.

Mimi took a long time to get changed. Adeline wondered if there were any ghosts in her room with her. She hoped not, as at least one of them seemed intent on hurting her. Adeline still couldn't figure out their role in all of this. Mimi clearly wasn't cursed – unless you called having a controlling boyfriend like Hadley a curse – but the ghosts… that was a supernatural oddity Adeline had yet to figure out.

Coco propped his head on her feet, his little eyebrows raised as he watched her. Something crashed down on the floor above their heads. Adeline started upright. What were the ghosts playing at now?

Coco didn't bark, but he jumped up from the couch and ran towards the stairs. When Adeline didn't immediately follow, he ran back to her and nudged at her leg making sure she was coming.

"It's okay, puppy," she said, patting his head. But he didn't settle. He ran back to the stairs again then dashed between them and Adeline.

"Okay, I hear you."

Coco circled around coming to stand beside her. He remained in that position as she made her way up the stairs, his little face looking up at her every so often to check she was okay. She patted his head, reassuring herself as much as him.

When she got upstairs, her pace quickened. The hall cabinet, which she kept bedlinen in, had toppled over. It lay on its side, blocking the door to Mimi's room. Tell-tale wisps of smoke told Adeline exactly how it had fallen.

"Adeline?" Mimi hammered on the inside of the door. "Adeline, I'm stuck!"

"There's something blocking the door," Adeline called to her. "Can you push against it?"

Mimi thumped against the door, but the cabinet didn't budge. "No, I can't get out!" Mimi frantically rattled the handle, but it was useless.

"I know." Adeline could hear the panic rising in Mimi's voice. "It's okay, I'm going to try and move it."

"No! You can't while you're pregnant."

Adeline blinked. She'd thought Mimi had suspected about her pregnancy, but she hadn't realised she was so certain. Had Hemi said something? Regardless, Adeline was determined to move the cabinet. A small stubborn part of her wouldn't let Bump be a reason not to try. She placed her hand on her stomach and thought she felt a kick in response. Bump agreed, it seemed.

She pushed her back against the end of the cabinet, bracing her feet against the wall. "It's okay. I think I can do it," she called to Mimi.

"Adeline!" Mimi's voice was a wail. "Don't be stupid. Hemi will kill me if you hurt yourself."

Adeline rolled her eyes. She was used to Hemi's over-protectiveness, and he was well used to her stubbornness. "I can deal with Hemi. It's fine, I can move the cabinet."

"You can't!" Mimi's voice was nearly a shriek now, and Adeline had a feeling her insistence was more to do with her panic than any real fear for Adeline's wellbeing. "Hemi told me I could only stay if I didn't stress you out. He says you always try to do more than you're really capable of…"

That was just the motivation Adeline needed. She shunted herself backwards taking the cabinet with her. As her knees straightened, the cabinet moved back just enough that they could get the door open a crack.

Coco immediately tried to squeeze through the gap, only succeeding in getting his head through. Mimi patted him, and he licked her hands, doing all he could to calm her.

Mimi peered at Adeline from inside the room. Her face was half made up, one eye perfectly winged, the other eyeliner-free. Her mascara on the winged side had run a little, stress tears overflowing. She seemed calmer, now that she could see out, even if she was still trapped.

"Are you okay? Are you hurt?"

Mimi shook her head. "I'm fine, just stuck." She bit her lip. "I… I shouldn't have said any of that."

Adeline gave a half-laugh. "*Hemi* shouldn't have said any of that."

"To be fair, he only said the bit about not stressing you out recently. The stuff about you being stubborn… that was from way back when you first started dating."

That made sense. That had been one of the first arguments she and Hemi had ever had. They'd mostly worked through it now. She'd got better at asking for help, and he'd got better at waiting until she did.

Adeline gave a half-laugh. "What did he think you were going to do to stress me out?"

"I don't know. Everything?" Mimi shrugged. "I think that was more about me than it was about you."

Adeline noticed Mimi's eyes flicking to Adeline's stomach. "But he told you I was pregnant?"

Mimi shook her head. "No, he didn't say anything about that. I just have a knack for picking pregnancies. It sounds weird, I know." Mimi shook her head as if she was embarrassed by that admission.

"It sounds a lot less weird than you think."

Mimi gestured towards Adeline's stomach. "Plus, it's pretty obvious when you're not wearing giant clothes."

Adeline glanced down and smoothed her T-shirt over Bump. The curve of her stomach was rather noticeable. She was finding it harder not to touch her belly in public too, enjoying the feeling of running her hand over it and imagining Bump's head on the other side.

She looked up, meeting Mimi's eye. They stared at each other, and both slowly smiled. "Let's get you out of there."

"Yes, please!"

Adeline couldn't get the cabinet to move any further, but with her pulling and Mimi pushing they managed to open the door enough for Mimi to squeeze out.

Coco pounced on her as soon as she was free. Mimi dropped into a crouch, letting him lick her face as she gave him all the pats. She looked up at Adeline. "Thank you."

Adeline shook her head, brushing away the praise. "Don't mention it. I'm sorry that happened to you."

Mimi frowned at the cabinet. "How did it happen? That thing is pretty solid. Was there an earthquake, or…" Mimi trailed off, and her face paled. She stood suddenly. "I should finish getting ready. I—"

Adeline put her hand out, stopping Mimi from squeezing back into her room. "You're not going out tonight, Mimi."

Mimi frowned as if she was going to argue, then her face crumpled. She let out a breath that was somewhere between a sigh and a sob. Adeline stepped towards her, resting her hand on Mimi's shoulder.

"It's okay," Adeline told her. "We're going to figure this out."

Adeline called Hadley, telling him Mimi wasn't feeling well and wouldn't be coming out. Even over the phone, she could feel him attempting to work some kind of magic on her. She used her own in return, persuading him it was a good idea to let Mimi rest. She was sure he'd have turned up on their doorstep to "help" otherwise.

Twenty minutes later, she and Mimi sat on the couch eating the heated-up risotto, Coco between them. The rice was a little gluggy from having been left sitting on the stove for so long, but the flavours were good.

"Is that why you've been hiding in your room?" Adeline asked. "Because you didn't want to stress me out?"

Mimi made a gesture with her head that was somewhere between a nod and a shake. "Maybe. Yeah... Well, that and..."

"That and the curse?"

Mimi's eyes widened, then she looked away quickly. She didn't get angry or run off this time though. That was progress.

"I don't think you're cursed, Mimi." Adeline thought of using magic to help persuade Mimi her words were the truth, but somehow it didn't feel right. Mimi had been magically manipulated enough lately as it was.

"You don't?" Mimi looked up at her.

Once upon a time, Adeline's family had thought they were cursed. She'd ended up cut off from her relatives, cut off from the magic... it was pure luck that Clara had found her, and helped her put the pieces back together.

But that would be too much for Mimi to take in right now. Adeline had to keep her explanation simple, so she didn't completely lose Mimi's trust.

"I think you're dating a guy who is very powerful, and very much an asshole."

Mimi frowned. "Hadley? But he's the one who's been helping me every time..." Something seemed to happen then, almost as if the threads of the spells Hadley had wound around Mimi were unravelling. Understanding slowly dawned on her face, and a hot red flushed into her cheeks. "Hadley," she said, the name sounding more like a swear word than anything Adeline had ever heard her say.

Mimi's eyelids flickered and then she shook her head. "But, no… strange things started happening before I started dating him. Right from when I first moved in with Nana Tui."

Adeline hesitated. Explaining about Hadley had been the relatively easy part. She wasn't sure how Mimi would take the next bit.

"Ghosts," she blurted out.

Mimi stared at her. "Ghosts?"

Adeline may just as well have started spouting about being a witch. She shook her head, wondering if it was too late to backtrack.

"What makes you think it's ghosts?" Mimi's tone was understandably dubious, but she still wasn't turning away. Adeline saw the hint of something in her eyes – not belief, exactly, but curiosity perhaps. That was something she could work with.

"Your grandma saw them, didn't she?"

Mimi shook her head. "Nana Tui was crazy. She used to say all sorts of things like that, but none of it was true."

"Hemi seems to think it was."

"And… you do too?"

Adeline hesitated. It was still strange for her to talk openly about this kind of thing, despite it having been a part of her life since she was a child. Before Clara and Hemi, she hadn't really talked to anyone about it. She'd never felt the need. Well, that wasn't true. She had tried a few times, and no one had believed her, just like Mimi hadn't believed her grandmother. But this time, Mimi really did need to take it seriously, and the only way that was going to happen was if Adeline was honest.

"The thing is," she said slowly, "*I* see ghosts. I have since I was a child."

Mimi frowned. She shifted as if she would get up and walk away, then stopped herself. She studied Adeline's face. Adeline understood what must be going through her mind. She was sure she must have looked the same when Clara told her she was a witch. The internal battle was obvious, as she tried to fit what she knew of the world with what Adeline was saying.

"And you think that that's what's happening here?" Mimi said finally. "You think ghosts are following me?"

"I know they are. I've seen them."

As Adeline spoke, a ghost appeared beside Mimi. Adeline watched Mimi's expression. It was clear Mimi couldn't *see* the ghost, but she was growing uneasy, anyway. Her eyes kept flicking to the side, looking for something. She may not be able to physically see the ghosts, but it was obvious she could still sense them.

"There's a man with a thin moustache next to you," Adeline said carefully. "He's been hanging around for a few days, along with several others."

Mimi stood, her face washing pale again. "That's not funny. Stop it."

Adeline stood too. "I'm not joking, Mimi. I'm trying to—"

Mimi shook her head, turning away from Adeline. Suddenly, the ghost rushed towards her. Adeline gasped, stepping in front of Mimi. The ghost ignored Adeline, rushing straight through her, his hand reaching for Mimi's throat.

Mimi shrank back, cowering against the wall. "What's happening?"

The furniture around them began to rumble, and Mimi screamed. Coco growled. Recognising Mimi's distress, he placed himself between the ghost and her. The ghost still didn't register Adeline's presence, but he sure recognised Coco. He reeled back, disappearing into the air as he did.

Adeline crouched beside Mimi. "It's okay, he's gone."

"Who *is* he?" Mimi peered up at Adeline, her fear making her look childlike.

"I honestly don't know." She wished she had more of an answer. "Normally, I can talk to the ghosts, but these ones don't even seem to know that I'm here." She didn't tell Mimi some of them didn't have faces. That part was excessively creepy, even when you were used to seeing spirits. "They're very focused on you," she said instead.

"But why?" Mimi's exhaustion was spelt out over her face. Adeline suddenly realised how long Mimi must've been struggling with this, with no one to talk to. No wonder she had felt cursed.

She took Mimi's hand, squeezing it. "I don't know what's going on, but I promise you we will figure it out."

Coco licked Mimi's face and wagged his tail as if promising too. Together, they would put a stop to this, even if they still weren't quite sure what "this" was.

CHAPTER ELEVEN

*B*y the end of Hemi's shift that night, Adeline and Mimi had formulated a plan. The ghosts had started bothering Mimi when she'd been living at her nan's house, or at least that's what Mimi thought. Given she couldn't see them, there was a fair bit of guesswork involved. Nana Tui had seen ghosts, though, so it was a good place to start.

Adeline and Hemi both had leave coming up already. Now, she and Mimi just had to persuade him to use it on a road trip. Adeline didn't think it would take much convincing. He was always up for getting out on the road and visiting family.

Hemi arrived home just after 3 a.m. He dropped his bag on a chair and looked between Mimi and Adeline. "What's going on?" he asked.

Mimi and Adeline weren't kidding themselves that the two of them sitting up, chatting, in the early hours of the morning didn't look suspicious, so they didn't bother with any pretences. Mimi handed him a bowl of hot risotto, and Adeline explained what they knew so far. As predicted, Hemi was on board with the plan of heading up north. He was rather keen on punching Hadley in the face first, but Adeline quickly persuaded him that wasn't the priority right now.

He and Mimi got to work planning. "I'll call my boss – see if I can start my leave early."

"Yeah, I'll do the same in the morning." Adeline should probably call Dana and offer an apology as well. She knew her friend wouldn't hold it against her, but she hated the way she had spoken earlier.

"I'll make us some snacks for the road," Mimi offered.

Adeline had to admit, she was less enthusiastic than the others about the road trip part, given car sickness and morning sickness wasn't exactly the world's best combination, but she was keen on the prospect of heading north.

"Have you ever been up to Nana Tui's place?" Mimi asked her.

Adeline nodded. "Yeah, when we were kids." She wished she'd known at the time that Nana Tui saw ghosts as well. She wasn't sure whether she would have opened up if she had known, but it would have been nice to at least meet another person who experienced the same kind of things she did.

Mimi glanced at her phone. "What's the time? You think we could head off now?" she asked.

Hemi tilted his head in a way that told Adeline he was considering it, but she shook her head firmly. "No, it's still too dark." The sun would be up soon, but Adeline didn't fancy several hours of driving through the gloomy streets until then.

Mimi and Hemi both sagged, but Hemi nodded, agreeing with Adeline's sentiment. "True. We can wait until morning proper."

Adeline could understand their excitement though, and if her witchy powers had extended to night-vision she would have been amped up for getting on the road as soon as possible too. "We'll go first thing," she told them. "But right now, we all need to at least try get some sleep."

They all dutifully headed upstairs, but Adeline had a feeling it would take more than a witchy intention to make slumber a reality tonight.

True to her word, Adeline had them up and out the door early the next morning, all of them rubbing the sleep from their eyes. Coco bounded into the front footwell of the car, excited about the prospect of a trip. Hemi had offered to do the driving, but they were taking Mimi's car, thank goodness. As much as it made Adeline smile that Hemi had held onto his tiny, teenage car all these years, she was decidedly less enthusiastic about the prospect of sitting squished up in a mini for several hours.

"When did you first notice the ghosts?" Hemi asked once they were on the road.

Mimi shrugged. "When I moved in, I think."

"Why did you move in there?" Adeline hoped the question wasn't too personal. She got the sense Mimi had moved around quite a bit over the years.

"I was between flats, and Auntie floated the idea of me looking after Nana Tui. It worked well at first... but then she became too unwell to stay at home."

Something crossed Mimi's face, and she fell quiet. Hemi and Adeline did too. Adeline hadn't been around at that point, but she knew how much he'd loved his nan. She reached out, squeezing his arm. He gave her a half-smile but kept his eyes on the road.

"I didn't have anywhere else to go, so I stayed on anyway," Mimi said quietly. "Then I found out she'd left me the house in her will... I don't know if I'll keep it though. I've been thinking a lot about selling."

Hemi frowned at this suggestion, and Adeline could tell he felt exactly the same way she did about it. It was Mimi's decision, but it seemed such a big thing to part with. The house was so entwined with Nana Tui and the family.

"I guess she left me the ghosts too," Mimi added.

"Did she ever say anything about them?" Adeline asked. "Ever tell you anything about who they were?" Adeline wasn't sure if it would make a difference. Most of the ghosts she saw were people she'd never known.

"She wasn't exactly lucid by the time she went into

hospital." Mimi paused, then frowned and shook her head slightly.

"What is it?" Adeline asked.

"No, it's nothing." Mimi hesitated again. "I was just thinking about some of the things she kept saying."

Adeline got a tingly witchy feeling at that. "Like what?"

"She said something about no one wanting to talk to her. We thought she was talking about the neighbours, or her friends, you know… we thought she was lonely."

"But now you're wondering if she meant the ghosts?"

"Yeah…" Mimi frowned. "I mean, if the ghosts don't seem to be able to see you, maybe they couldn't see her either?"

Adeline nodded. "It's possible." It still didn't explain why they seemed so fixated on Mimi. If she hadn't been able to see ghosts before – and still couldn't see them now – why were they so interested in trying to get her attention?

"We should have tried to understand her more." Hemi frowned at the road ahead and Adeline could see his fingers were tightening on the wheel. Mimi looked down at her hands, pressing them together in her lap. The guilt in the car was palpable, both of them blaming themselves for something that wasn't their fault. Perhaps this was what the ghosts were attaching to.

Adeline squeezed Hemi's shoulder again, gently. "You couldn't have known. She wasn't well."

Hemi let out a breath slowly, and his face cleared a

little. "But maybe we can help her now. I mean… not help *her* but figure out what was wrong."

Adeline nodded. She'd never been more determined to make sure one of their ghost hunting expeditions went well. "We will. I promise."

The rest of the drive up was quiet. Hemi concentrated on the road, and Adeline and Mimi both napped on and off, lost in their own thoughts.

"We should visit your mum on the way back down," Mimi said, as they passed the sign welcoming them into Hastings.

Hemi frowned at the road and for a moment Adeline thought he was going to pretend he hadn't heard. "Maybe," he said finally.

No ghosts had climbed into the car with them – *thank goodness*, Adeline thought to herself – but they had reappeared at different points along the journey. When they stopped for a pee break, Adeline saw a familiar wispy figure floating outside Mimi's stall. She decided not to mention it to Mimi… mainly because she knew how awkward she would feel if it were her. Who would want to know they were being watched by a spirit while they peed?

Once they set out again, Adeline dozed for a while, as did Coco, leaning heavily against her legs. She'd have to get Hemi to take him for a big run when they got to Hastings. Being cramped up in the car all morning was not exactly ideal – for the humans or the canines.

Hemi's grandmother's place was exactly as Adeline remembered it, bar the indoor plants hanging from the ceiling. She guessed they'd had to come down now there was no one to water them. The garden more than made up for that, though. It was wild and overgrown, but Adeline could sense an energy to it. The flowerbeds all had a sense of... *purpose* to them as if the plants knew exactly what they were doing. Adeline couldn't help questioning whether Hemi's grandmother had in fact been a witch. She supposed it didn't matter either way. A witch by any other name is just as magical. Adeline didn't say that thought aloud to the others, but she was quietly pleased with it.

The porch was strung with windchimes and other hanging ornaments. Suddenly, it made sense why Mimi had wanted to have one up at their place, but a pit formed in Adeline's stomach. Were these ones spelled too?

Adeline touched one of them, but there was no vibrating hum coming off it. If anything, the air around them felt flat... heavy. She couldn't quite explain the sensation. The closest word she could come up with was "numb" but how could something made of metal feel numb? At any rate, she couldn't sense any immediately dangerous magic.

Inside was the familiar mix of colour and chaos that Adeline remembered. She let out a breath. Strangely, the chaos made her feel calm. It was exactly what she wanted in a home. She hoped that her baby's life could be filled with just as much colour and magic and whimsy as they'd found right here.

"So, what exactly are we looking for?" Hemi asked. Mimi turned to Adeline as well, eagerly awaiting her guidance.

Adeline wished she had something more concrete for them, but instead, she just shrugged. "I don't know, really. Anything ghost-related I guess?"

Mimi visibly sagged, obviously looking for something more certain.

"I could try a location spell type thing." Adeline still hadn't quite got a handle on the language. She thought of everything as "witchy business", rather than knowing what was a spell or an incantation. "I haven't done one before, so I might need to call Clara for help..." Adeline trailed off, suddenly realising she hadn't even told her cousin they were heading out of town. Hopefully, Clara would see the funny side of it.

"Don't accuse me of fussing, but..." Hemi stopped himself, perhaps reconsidering.

Adeline smiled and squeezed his arm, thankful for his gentle way of looking after her. "I do need to rest first, yes."

He smiled back, relieved he didn't have to convince her.

Mimi nodded. "Yeah, true. I'm pretty tired as well."

That wasn't surprising, given how little sleep they'd gotten last night. Perhaps a nap would do them all some good. Besides, spending some time in the house might help Adeline get a feel for what she was looking for.

"I'll stay in my old room," Mimi said. "Do you two want to take the guest bedroom?"

"Oo… sharing a bed under my grandmother's roof? Scandalous." Hemi winked at Adeline and nudged her shoulder.

Adeline touched her stomach. "Um… I think we're well past that, babe."

Hemi put his arm around her and kissed the side of her head. "Nana Tui would be so happy about Bump," he told her.

Adeline hoped that was true. She felt a kinship with his grandma, knowing they'd shared the secret of seeing ghosts. She just hoped she could fix whatever it was that had gone wrong to make them stop seeing her.

CHAPTER TWELVE

*D*espite being the only one who was pregnant and chronically ill, Adeline was the first to wake up from their nap. She headed downstairs, letting Hemi keep resting. She sat out on the porch, watching the sun dip down behind the hills, miles of green stretching out around her. This was one thing she wished she had in the city, the expanse of nature. Wellington had plenty of green spaces, you just had to work a little harder to get to them, and the sound of traffic often followed you.

Coco raced around the yard, sniffing everything in sight. He loved going new places, and Adeline wondered if this could become a regular thing, bringing him up here once they'd sorted out the ghost problem. He ran back to her, checking she was still okay.

"Go on," she told him. "You can play in the garden."

Coco didn't need any more encouragement. He raced

off, eagerly sniffing and peeing on all the plants. Adeline laughed. Oh, for the happy life of a dog!

Footsteps padding through the house made her turn, and then Mimi appeared on the deck.

"Hey," she said, rubbing her eyes. "I swear I never sleep during the day normally."

"You must have needed it."

"Yeah." Mimi stared out at the sunset, just as Adeline had done, then settled herself onto the porch swing. Adeline joined her, and she felt them both relaxing, matching their inhales to the gentle motion of the swing.

There was a light breeze, and Adeline watched the windchimes swaying back and forth. A light clinking came from the chimes, each time the pipes hit each other, but it wasn't the musical chaos Adeline had been expecting. "These ones don't make much noise," she said.

Mimi gave a short laugh. "Yeah, sorry about that. I wanted you to have one, but I had no idea how loud it would be. I guess that's Wellington wind for you."

Adeline stared at the windchimes on the porch. "Maybe…" More likely, magic was playing a part in that.

Mimi shivered suddenly, perhaps remembering that the windchime had reappeared in the back garden above the bones. Hadley certainly knew how to create a spectacle – a horribly creepy one at that.

They sat in silence again, but the peaceful moment had broken. Adeline could feel something building between them, all the unsaid thoughts wanting to burst out.

"Even if we don't figure out what's going on with the ghosts," Mimi started, "thank you for trying to help me."

"Of course. You're family."

Mimi stared out at the garden, worrying at her lip with her teeth. "I haven't exactly been treating you like it this week, though."

Adeline didn't say anything at first. She had been uncomfortable with the way Mimi had behaved, but she wondered if that was almost what *made* them family. The fact that they could see each other at their worst, and still stick around.

"You've been going through a lot," she said finally. "I understand."

Mimi gave a half-smile, still not ready to let her guilt go. "Whatever happens, I'm going to be the best auntie/cousin to that little baby of yours."

Adeline smiled. She touched her stomach protectively. It felt weird to have someone other than Hemi mention her pregnancy aloud.

Mimi hesitated then frowned. "Can I ask you something?"

"Yeah, of course."

"Why don't you want anyone to know?"

Adeline blinked. She thought of spouting what she had been saying to Hemi the last few months, that it was too early to tell people, but it wasn't. She was well into her second trimester, nearing her third. It was obvious she was pregnant. But still... something was holding her back.

"I guess I'm scared," Adeline admitted.

"Of what?"

Adeline shrugged. "Of something going wrong?" She frowned. That wasn't all, though. There was something else niggling at her. Her health had actually been surprisingly good. Apart from the tiredness, and her blood pressure being a bit wonky, she'd been really well during her pregnancy. She hadn't had a major seizure since Christmas Eve, and only a few smaller ones since.

"I think… I think I'm scared that I won't be a good mum," Adeline said.

Mimi's hand moved to her lips automatically. She shook her head, almost seeming like she was going to cry. "Adeline… you have to know that's not true."

Adeline shrugged. Until she said the words, she hadn't even been conscious that that was what she was thinking. But now she'd spoken them, she couldn't deny they were true. "I don't know. I guess… it's been so long since I had a family. My parents died when I was young, and I've never been around kids that much. I love them, but…" Adeline trailed off, emotion choking her words. She thought of the little boy and girl in the park, and how awkward she had been around them. Had she always been like that with children? Honestly, she didn't know.

She pressed her hands to her stomach, imagining Bump's head on the other side. She wanted to be a good mum to her baby; she just didn't know if she had enough inside her to make that happen.

Mimi let out a breath. She sank back against the seat and stared at the setting sun. Adeline joined her. There was something so calming about watching the light refract into the clouds making a beautiful watercolour painting of peach and gold and pink and blue. Coco trotted over to them, perhaps recognising Adeline was upset.

Adeline reached out, patting him. "Good boy, Coco. Good boy," she said.

"They say having a dog is like having a toddler," Mimi said.

Adeline glanced at her. "Yeah, that's true, I guess." Adeline did spend a lot of time persuading Coco not to eat things he shouldn't or go into places where he was going to get stuck. "But Coco looks after me too. It won't be the same with a baby. What if I'm sick all the time?"

Mimi clucked her tongue. "Well, you *are* lucky enough to have a paramedic as a partner."

Adeline chuckled. "You're right, I am." Adeline wouldn't be alone in this. Hemi would always be by her side, and she had a team of supportive friends and work-mates who would be more than willing to babysit and get baby cuddles. Not to mention Clara, and Hemi's family. They would all be there with her through this.

"What if I collapse while I'm holding the baby?" Adeline's voice dropped to a croak, barely able to get the words out. This was her biggest fear. She'd barely been able to make herself hold Caleb, and that was with Dana and Talia standing by. What if she couldn't pick up her own child?

Mimi reached for her, squeezing her arm tight.

Adeline leaned into the touch, letting it ground her. "Adeline, do you really think any of us would let you fall? Coco warns you before anything happens, right? He'll be the best dog-brother a kid could ask for."

That was true. Apart from the broken wrist at Christmas, Adeline hardly ever had injuries from her seizures or low blood pressure these days. Even at Christmas, that had only been because she'd been standing on a staircase at the time and hadn't been able to get to a safe place quickly enough.

"Besides," Mimi said. "I've been behaving like a naughty teenager this week, and you've handled that just fine." Mimi flashed Adeline a grin and they both laughed.

"I wouldn't exactly say you've been behaving like a teenager."

"But close to it?"

"Close to it." Adeline laughed.

The woman beside her didn't feel like a teenager now. This was the first time Adeline felt like they had any kind of connection. Maybe this was another part of being a family. You didn't always immediately get on with everybody, but you could build the relationships if you tried. Adeline could see Mimi becoming a friend eventually – someone her baby would absolutely adore.

Mimi cleared her throat. "I don't mean to rush you, but..."

"Any leads on the ghosts?" Adeline nodded slowly, though she wasn't entirely sure if she was saying yes. Something was starting to come together in her mind, but she wasn't quite ready to share it yet. "How did you meet Hadley?" she asked instead.

Mimi blinked, clearly not expecting the change of subject, though Adeline was becoming more and more sure it wasn't *really* a change of subject.

"He owns the hardware store in town – does odd jobs for people on the side. He came out to fix something for Nana Tui, and I met him then."

Adeline frowned. Somehow that didn't fit with the picture she had in her head of Hadley. With that charm magic of his, she'd expected some smarmy career for him – something where he manipulated and beguiled people – not going door to door helping people out.

"I know," Mimi said as if she'd read all that on Adeline's face. "Not what you'd expect, right? I think he inherited the shop from his dad."

That made sense. People ended up in all sorts of family businesses, whether or not it suited them.

"Anyway, I didn't think much of him when I met him. Nana Tui actually warned me off him. Apparently, he has a history of being pushy with women, but…" Mimi trailed off. She frowned as if puzzled by her own words. "Honestly, I'm not exactly sure when that changed. Nana Tui and I were both adamant I wasn't going to go out with him, and then…"

Magic, Adeline thought. Mimi hadn't been interested in him, and then suddenly she was, probably right around the time Hadley started using his charm on her.

Mimi shook her head. "Anyway, some… stuff…

happened. And then Nana Tui went downhill really quickly. I guess he was there for me, and I started relying on him. That probably sounds terrible." Mimi's cheeks flushed, shame colouring them, but Adeline shook her head.

"No, you're not the one in the wrong here." Adeline ran Mimi's story through in her mind. There was something missing, some piece she couldn't quite put together. It felt close though. She could almost see it.

"Tell me about the *stuff*," she said gently.

Mimi visibly cringed. She turned her face away, not wanting to look at Adeline. Coco chose that moment to come bounding back to them. He lay on Mimi's feet, supporting her with his warmth.

"That's when things with the ghosts got worse," she said.

"You said something about it all happening again? When we found the bones."

Mimi nodded. "Yeah… I guess that was what started it all. It was after Nana Tui got sick. She wasn't making sense, kept rambling about no one being able to hear her, kept telling me Hadley was no good… which in hindsight I should have listened to." Mimi sighed. Her eyelashes flickered as if she was reliving the memory behind them. Adeline touched her hand but didn't say anything, not wanting to interrupt the story.

"Anyway, this one day was particularly bad, and I accidentally left the front door open. This bird got in…" Mimi hesitated. Each word seemed to strain from inside her as if she'd held on to this for so long, letting go of it caused her pain. "It was a fantail."

Adeline's stomach dropped. She knew the significance fantails held in Māori mythology. The fantail – pīwakawaka – responsible for the presence of death in the world. "You thought it meant your nan…"

Mimi nodded. "I was so scared, I tried to chase it out. It panicked and flew into the window. There were feathers everywhere. It only left when Hadley managed to capture it and set it free."

Adeline could see how it had happened. Hadley had been there for Mimi at a time when her world was tipping underneath her. He'd comforted her when her nan got sick and reassured her every time the ghosts caused something strange. No wonder she'd got caught under his spell.

"He's like that. He's so good when I'm upset. There was other stuff happening – strange noises, things moving… ghost stuff, I guess. Hadley was really good at calming me down."

"But things weren't great otherwise?"

Mimi shook her head. "He's so controlling. Every time I tried to do something different – something for myself – he'd get angry. I was thinking about breaking up with him, then the feathers started appearing."

"And after that, bones?" Adeline could see it all now. He wanted Mimi to need him and making her think she was cursed made her need him. It was sick – sick and manipulative.

"I'm so stupid," Mimi shook her head, tears threatening. "I should have known it was him."

Adeline put her arm around her. "How could you? Who expects their partner to do something like that? Besides, the ghosts by themselves are enough to frighten anyone."

Mimi nodded. She wiped her face, seeming to gain strength with the action. "What do we do about the ghosts? Please tell me you've thought of something."

Adeline nodded. "I'm working on it. I think we should eat first."

"There's no food in the house." Mimi hesitated. "But I could drive into town and get some... you and Hemi need to talk, I think."

Adeline sighed. With everything that had happened, she and Hemi had never resolved the argument they'd had before Coco choked on the bone. "I guess it's the day for deep and meaningfuls."

Coco wagged his tail, agreeing with the sentiment.

CHAPTER THIRTEEN

Hemi was in the kitchen when Adeline got back inside. He nodded his head towards Mimi's departing figure. "That looked serious?" he said.

"Yeah, it kind of was."

"Anything I should be worried about?" Hemi looked like he was already worrying, whether or not Adeline said he should.

She shrugged. "Hadley's even worse than we thought."

Hemi nodded as if he'd half expected that anyway. "That guy…" He shook his head. "I just wish I'd known."

"Me too." Not that it would have made much difference, Adeline thought. If Hadley's magic had taken her in, despite her being a witch, neither Hemi nor Mimi would have stood a chance.

Hemi chewed on his lip, watching Adeline. "Adey, are we okay?"

Adeline swallowed. As much as she had said it was a

day for deep and meaningfuls, right now she wanted to do anything other than have this conversation. "Mimi's giving us some space. We need to talk."

Hemi nodded, slowly. His eyes avoided hers for a moment, then he tilted his head towards the living room. "Come sit with me?"

They made their way to the couch, each taking an end of it and curling their legs up so they could sit facing each other. It was a good idea to come in here, Adeline decided. She felt calmer in amongst the colours and life of the room, just as she and Mimi had felt more relaxed looking out over the garden and the sunset.

Coco made his way inside and climbed up onto Adeline. "Oof, puppy, you are not a lap dog!"

He made a happy little grunt and settled on her lap anyway. *Keeping me in place*, Adeline thought to herself. Coco felt they needed to have this conversation too.

"I'm sorry I haven't been around much lately," Hemi started. "I shouldn't have dumped my cousin on you, then disappeared."

Adeline shook her head. "Babe, I know you were on nights. It's not your fault."

"Yeah, but I said I would talk to Mimi, and I didn't. You told me she needed help, and I didn't listen."

Adeline nodded, accepting the apology. To be fair, she should have kept up her end of that. She'd intended to wait for Hemi, but instead, she'd gone barrelling in there, trying to force Mimi to talk before she was ready.

"I shouldn't have pushed," she said. "I've not been great

at communicating lately." It all came back to communication, she realised. All of the problems she'd had lately – with Mimi and Hemi, with the ghosts, even with Dana – it had come down to not being able to say what she really needed to.

"Are you really happy I can't talk to the ghosts anymore?"

Hemi's expression fell. "Babe…" He ran his hands down his face and shook his head. "Sometimes it's hard, yeah?"

Adeline swallowed. This wasn't what she wanted to hear, but she nodded, doing her best to let him say his piece without interrupting.

"It's not that I wish *you* were more normal – you *are* normal, in your own weird way. It's just…" Hemi reached for her hands, and she let him. Of course, Coco felt he had to be a part of that and started licking both of their palms.

Hemi gave a half-laugh, wiping the slobber off on Coco's fur. "It's just, I see what it does to you. You get so stressed and so *tired*. When I woke up the other night, after the ghosts on the doorstep, you looked terrified. You were so pale, and…" Hemi shook his head again. "There's nothing I can do. I don't know how to make it better."

Adeline saw the night through his eyes. She'd screamed when he came downstairs, utter panic filling her thinking he was another ghost. "You hugged me," she said.

"Huh?"

"When you came downstairs. You hugged me. You made it better." She took his hand again, and this time

Coco let them have the moment. "You know, I always think of our ghost hunting adventures as like our date nights."

Hemi blinked. "Really?"

"Really. You can't see the ghosts, but you help me through all of it."

"I'd do anything for you, Adey… but only if you want me to." He grinned, and Adeline laughed.

"Besides, if I couldn't see ghosts, I would never have figured out what was going on with Mimi."

"True." Hemi hesitated, then took a breath. "Are you two okay? I know things have been a bit… I feel like a dick for just lumping you together when you weren't getting along."

Adeline smiled. For once, the answer to that question made her happy rather than want to tear her hair out. "We're okay. We had a good talk. She told me she thinks I'll make a good mum."

Hemi raised his eyebrows. He opened his mouth to speak, then closed it again and frowned. "Was that in question?" he asked finally.

Adeline shrugged. "Maybe. I don't know."

Hemi scootched towards her, wrapping her in a hug. "You, Adeline Wilson, are going to be the best mum."

Adeline rested her head against his chest. She could hear his heartbeat, and that was even more reassuring than his words. He would be a great dad, and they would do it together.

"I'm glad you told her," Hemi said quietly.

Adeline could hear the relief in his voice. She almost didn't want to set him straight, but she had to be honest. "I didn't tell her; she guessed." Just like Clara, Dana, and everyone else at work had guessed. Adeline couldn't keep pretending no one knew.

"Speaking of mums…" Adeline pulled back to look at him. "Why are you avoiding yours?"

Hemi blinked. He opened his mouth as if he was going to protest, claim he hadn't avoided every phone call from his mum and changed the subject every time she was brought up for the last couple of months. Instead, he shook his head. "I'm not. Well, I am…"

Adeline tipped her head to the side, giving him her best sceptical look. He let out a breath. "You're right. I am. I guess I just find it hard. To not tell her, I mean. I've never kept secrets from her."

He had to be the only adult she knew who genuinely meant that. He'd never lied to his mum, even when they were teenagers.

Adeline closed her eyes for a moment. She hadn't thought about how hard this was for him – how much she had asked by making him keep the secret. Hemi's hands still rested on her shoulders, and she felt the warmth of them giving her strength. She took a slow breath, and she could feel him doing the same. Both of them in sync, both of them working as a team.

She opened her eyes. She gave Hemi a smile. "Let's go see her on the way back home." She took his hand, pressing it gently to her stomach, connecting both of them to Bump. Coco raised his head, snuffling Adeline's belly, his tail dancing in excitement at the prospect of the little one inside. "I think it's time your mum knows about her mokopuna."

A slow smile spread across Hemi's face. "Are you sure?"

Adeline nodded. "I'm sure."

"Then we better solve this ghost mystery ASAP." Hemi's smile turned into a grin.

Adeline couldn't help but grin back. "You got it."

"Though… I really think we better come up with some better ideas for date nights. What do other couples do? Flower arranging? Ten-pin bowling?"

Adeline laughed. "Maybe we just make a point to cook together more often? We could do weekend brunches when you're on late shifts?"

"I'd love that." Hemi pulled her into a hug again. Coco's tail thumped, happy now his humans were getting along.

"Speaking of the ghosts…" Hemi asked. "Any progress on that?"

"Not yet, but I have an idea." Adeline leaned back to look at Hemi. "I think I need your help though."

She hadn't thought it was possible, but Hemi's grin stretched even further.

"I love it when you say that."

Hemi stood balanced on top of the rail that ran around the edge of the porch. Adeline could see he was getting exasperated, as he tried to hook down the windchimes, but he was trying not to let it show. He was probably just so relieved that she'd asked him, rather than climbing up there herself, that he wasn't going to spoil things by complaining. He finally managed to hook the last of the windchimes down and handed it to Adeline.

"Best boyfriend ever?" He flashed her a cheeky grin.

Adeline grinned back. "Maybe," she said. "Let's see if I was right first."

Hemi hopped down and together they examined the windchimes.

"They weren't making any noise," Adeline told him.

"Okay…"

Adeline sighed, realising she would have to explain a little more. She was so used to Hemi being on her same wavelength that sometimes she forgot he didn't actually live inside her head. "There was some kind of spell on the one Mimi put up at home. These ones don't *feel* spelled, or at least not in the same way, but the ghosts don't seem to be able to talk to me… or see me, I guess," she said. "And it seems like all of us have been having trouble saying what we really mean, so, that started me thinking, when the windchimes didn't make any noise—"

"That maybe there's a witchy intention behind it?"

"Exactly."

Adeline examined the windchimes. She hadn't seen all that many of them up close before, but this looked pretty standard to her. The one at home seemed to be spelled for Adeline to forget about it, so perhaps these were disguising their magic too.

Hemi frowned. "There is something stuffed inside."

Adeline turned the chime upside down and sure enough, the insides of the pipes were packed with paper. "An intention and an action," she said, pulling it out.

Hemi frowned. "But what exactly were they intending to do?"

Adeline shook her head. "I don't know. But I have a feeling Hadley's behind it."

"So, is it fixed by you pulling that out? Seems kind of anticlimactic."

Adeline didn't think he was really complaining about that, though. "No, unfortunately. It's never that simple to undo a spell. But it has got us one step closer to figuring out what the spell was."

Hemi frowned. "How exactly?"

Adeline smoothed out the paper, revealing a newspaper cutting with a photo of Hadley and another man. "Because that," Adeline said, pointing to the second man in the photo, "is the ghost."

CHAPTER FOURTEEN

Adeline and Hemi pulled all of the paper out of the windchimes and laid it flat on the table. Unfortunately, after being outside, scrunched up, in all weathers, the article that went with the picture of Hadley and the ghost was too smeared to read. All they could make out was Hadley's name and something about the hardware store.

The door clattered open, suddenly, making both of them jump. Mimi strode across the room, grocery bags bashing against furniture as she went.

"Hey, what's wrong?" Adeline took the bags from her, and Mimi's hands automatically flew to her face, palms pressing to her flushed cheeks.

She shook her head. "He's here. Somehow he's... I didn't tell him I was coming back, but he *knew*."

Hemi stood, moving towards Mimi as if ready to protect her. "What do you mean he's here?"

Mimi flopped down on the couch, laying her head back, still shaking it. Adeline dropped the groceries in the kitchen and then went to sit next to Mimi. Coco got up with her and laid his chin on Mimi's arm, offering support.

"I had to walk past the hardware store to get to the supermarket. I was expecting it to be closed, with Hadley in Wellington, but he was standing inside looking out, watching as if he was waiting for me."

Adeline and Hemi glanced at each other. Adeline could see his anger rising, but he pressed his lips together, trying to contain it. "I'm sorry," she said. "That's really creepy."

Mimi sat up, suddenly agitated. "It is, right? It's not just me?

"Definitely not."

"How did he know? I didn't tell him we were coming back; I didn't tell anyone! Was he watching the house? That's not just creepy, that's—"

"Illegal," Hemi finished for her. His tone was dark.

Adeline shifted uncomfortably. She didn't want to defend Hadley in any way, but she had a feeling he hadn't needed to watch the house to know what Mimi was doing. She glanced at Hemi. "Babe…" she said.

Hemi looked up at her and frowned, reading what she was thinking on her face. Hadley was using magic to track Mimi.

Mimi looked between the two of them. "What? What are you thinking?"

Hemi tilted his head in Mimi's direction, his eyebrows

raised. Adeline nodded. Mimi would be more likely to believe it coming from him. He had a way of making everything seem perfectly rational, even when it was anything but.

"Adeline doesn't just see ghosts," he said. "She's a witch. Hadley is too, as far as we can tell. He's been using magic on you – mostly to manipulate you – and we think that's why he knew where you were." Hemi kept his tone even, making it all sound as reasonable as he possibly could.

Even so, Adeline wanted to burst into a fit of giggles at how ridiculous it all sounded. Mimi frowned at him, waiting. Adeline didn't blame her. It sounded like Hemi had been building to a punchline, which never came. They had alluded to magic, talking about the ghosts and about the power Hadley seemed to have over Mimi, but there was something different about using the word "witch". Adeline had felt exactly the same when Clara had laid it all out for her too.

Mimi took a breath, but it hitched in her throat before she managed to form words. "I'm sorry, what?!" She looked from Hemi to Adeline. Adeline tried not to shrink under the scrutiny. "You're a witch?"

"Yes."

"And Hadley is…" Mimi's breath sped into little gasps, on the verge of a panic attack. "Hadley is…"

"It's okay." Adeline nearly poured a calming intention into the words, but Mimi had been spelled enough recently. "We're going to figure this out, I promise," she said instead. "It's all going to be okay."

Coco shifted his head, laying his chin on Mimi's lap, and his paw across her thigh. If he could have spoken, Adeline knew he would have been repeating the same words she was.

"I just… I just need a moment." Mimi stood, displacing Coco. She rubbed her temples hard as if she would wear through her skin, but then stopped, staring at the crumpled paper on the table.

Adeline looked at Hemi, and he gave her a nod, encouraging her to explain.

"We think it's a spell." If they were telling Mimi about witches, they may as well tell her everything. "We think maybe Hadley put those in the windchimes to make communication difficult between you and your grandmother… or something like that. We're not exactly sure what he was trying to do. But that's a picture of the ghost and… I don't know. I'm still trying to put it together."

Mimi's eyes were locked on the picture of Hadley and the ghost, but they shot up to meet Adeline's now. "That's the ghost?"

Adeline nodded. "One of them."

"It can't be." Mimi backed away. Her foot hit the edge of the rug, and she stumbled, letting out a scream. Hemi grabbed her before she fell, but it wasn't the stumble causing her to shriek. "It can't be," she said again, but she whispered it this time as if she already knew it was true.

"Do you know him?" Hemi said gently. "Who is he?"

Mimi looked back at the photograph, the movement so slow and tired her whole body seemed to drag with it. She picked up the paper, smoothing it out. "That's Hadley's father."

Adeline made tea, pouring every calming witchy intention she could muster into the action. They sat around the table, piecing together the bits of paper from the windchimes. Adeline didn't really believe it would tell them anything, but it was something they could do, and sometimes an action was all people needed to stay calm, whether or not it came with a magical intention behind it.

"Does this mean the other ghosts are Hadley's relatives too?" Mimi asked.

Adeline shook her head. "I don't know. Possibly." She didn't know why, but that didn't feel right. She still felt like the ghosts were attached to Mimi, not Hadley. "Do you know when his father passed away?"

Mimi shrugged. "Not exactly. Hadley was kind of funny about it – didn't tell me at the time. I think it was around the same time as Nana Tui, though."

"I know grief makes people do strange things, but not telling you…" Hemi cleared his throat. "That's a little weird, isn't it?"

Mimi nodded. "I thought so at the time. I'm supposedly the love of his life, and… oh cripes, you don't think he killed him, do you?"

They stared at each other, silence sticking in their

throats. Adeline wanted to reassure Mimi, but she couldn't honestly rule anything out at this stage.

"He didn't have a good relationship with his dad," Mimi said quietly, "but I never would have thought... Is that what this is? His dad returning as a vengeful spirit?"

"I don't think so," Adeline said hesitantly. It was more like the ghost was trying to help Hadley – playing into his mind games, so that Mimi felt scared and wanted Hadley nearby for comfort.

Adeline stared at the picture. The two men didn't smile, as you would expect them to in a photo for a newspaper. Hadley stared out at the camera. Creases in the paper lined his face, so his expression was hard to read, but even through time, Adeline could feel the arrogance coming off him. His father stared at him, not the camera, a slight frown on his face as if exasperated. This didn't seem like the type of relationship that would have a father coming back from the grave to help his son win over a girl.

Adeline mentally ran through the encounters she'd had with the ghosts, especially the ones where Hadley had been there.

"When the ghost hit you in the face with the glass," she said slowly, "you knew Hadley would be afraid of the blood."

Mimi blinked, then shook her head. "When the ghost what...?"

Adeline grimaced. She'd given Mimi an overview that the ghosts had been causing chaos in her life, but she hadn't given her specifics of everything she'd seen them do. "When you and Hadley were talking, the ghost shoved the glass at you. It made your lip bleed."

Mimi touched her mouth as if she thought she would find blood there now. "That was the ghost? I thought I was just clumsy."

"Well..." Hemi gave a cheeky grin.

"Shut up!" Mimi joined him with a half-hearted laugh.

"Anyway," Adeline interrupted. "Why would the ghost do that? The gaslighting I can understand – it made you call Hadley for comfort – but the smashed lip? It made him back off. If you knew he gets funny at the sight of blood, surely his father would?" The ghost had seemed so happy at the sight of Mimi injured – the memory of it still unsettled Adeline – but maybe there was something else behind it.

"Ghosts get confused sometimes, don't they?" Hemi asked. "Maybe he didn't know what he was doing?"

"Yeah, but all his actions are so purposeful. You've seen what Stanley gets like when he's..." Adeline trailed off, realising no, Hemi hadn't seen what Stanley was like, given he couldn't see him at all.

"So, what do you think the ghost was trying to do?" Hemi asked. "Is he just trying to hurt Mimi for the sake of it?"

Adeline's heart sank at the thought. She glanced at Mimi. Her face was drawn, and she didn't look up. "Surely it can't be that," Adeline said, with as much certainty as she could muster. Honestly, she wasn't certain of anything much right then.

"I met him a few times," Mimi said. "Jeffry, his name was. He was friends with Nana Tui. He was sweet. He used to bring her groceries."

That didn't sound like the type of person who would turn into a vengeful ghost. Hemi let out an exasperated puff of air. "So if he's not trying to hurt Mimi, and he's not trying to help Hadley… what on earth is he doing?"

Adeline shook her head. Figuring out who the ghost was had felt like a win, but now it seemed to have left them with more questions than answers.

Mimi sat up straight, suddenly. "I was going to go out again last night."

"Huh?"

"Before the cabinet fell, and I got trapped in my room, I was going back out to meet Hadley."

Hemi frowned. "And you think the ghost was trying to stop you?"

Mimi stood, her body needing to move as she pieced it together. "The blood on my lip drove Hadley away… The cabinet kept me from going to meet him… I think he's trying to stop Hadley!"

"Really?" Hemi frowned. "Why would he do that?"

Mimi stopped, her face falling. "I… don't know."

Now Adeline thought about it, the ghosts she'd seen the night Hadley left feathers on the doorstep could have been trying to warn her. One of them had even pointed, and it was almost like they had encouraged Coco to bark.

"I think you could be right. We don't know why, but that doesn't mean it's not true."

"So, what do we do now?" Hemi asked. "It's all very well if the ghosts are on our side, but we still can't talk to them, and Hadley's still—"

"Behaving like a creep," Mimi finished for him.

Mimi and Hemi turned towards Adeline. Once again, Adeline found them both staring at her, expecting her to have an answer. Once again, she didn't have a clue.

CHAPTER FIFTEEN

After another half hour of puzzling but getting nowhere, they decided to go back to Adeline's original plan of eating first and figuring out the ghosts later. Adeline and Mimi started dinner while Hemi took a moment to call his mum. Adeline could hear him from the living room, joking with her and trying to get her back onside while she chastised him for not calling more often. Even without being able to make out her words, Adeline could hear the admonishment in his mum's tone, along with her delight at finally hearing from him.

"I know, I know, Mum, but we're going to come see you real soon, okay?" Hemi walked past the kitchen doorway and winked at Adeline.

She grinned back, happy to see him relaxed now he knew he only had to keep the secret a few more days.

"Better be prepared, cuz." Mimi nudged Adeline's side.

"She is going to be all over you once she knows you're hapū."

Adeline ran her hand over Bump. She waited for the familiar wave of anxiety to crash over her, but it didn't come. Instead, she just felt warm inside… almost excited at the idea.

Mimi made her way around the kitchen, humming a tune as she cooked. Adeline had been worried telling Mimi about witches and ghosts would have had her curled up in a ball on the floor. Instead, it seemed to have calmed her. It must be a relief to know she wasn't cursed or crazy.

"Are you okay here if I go call my cousin?" Adeline asked. "I think she'll have more ideas than I do."

Mimi nodded. "Anything if it means we figure this out faster."

Adeline went out onto the porch to call. The line rang for a while before Clara answered, and Adeline wondered if her cousin was waiting for Lola to bring her the phone.

Finally, she picked up. "Hello?"

"Hey, it's me."

Clara's voice warmed when she recognised Adeline's. "Hey, stranger. I was wondering where you got to. Lola's been giving me all sorts of strange signals today."

That wasn't surprising. As magical as their assistance dogs were, there was still a limit to how much they could communicate when they couldn't speak. Lola would have struggled to spell out "Adeline and Coco have taken off on a spur-of-the-minute roadie" using only woofs and barks.

"Funny story," she told Clara. "We're actually in Hastings."

Clara chuckled. "Let me guess, you and Hemi are off chasing ghosts?"

"You guessed it."

"Anything useful?"

"Maybe. I definitely found evidence of a spell. Do you have time to chat now?"

"Always for you, Adeline."

Adeline gave her a rundown on everything she'd discovered since they last spoke. She found herself getting more and more angry with Hadley, as she recounted the story. How could he have thought it was okay to mess with Mimi like that? He claimed to love her, but all he was doing was controlling her. It was clear Mimi didn't love him back – why would he want to be with someone who was only with him because they were afraid?

"Hadley sounds like a right piece of work," Clara said when Adeline finished.

That was an understatement but coming from someone as restrained and well-spoken as Clara, it was quite the indictment.

"I think you're right about the paper in the wind-chimes having started this. Seems like Hadley's diving into witchy business but doesn't really know what he's doing."

Adeline couldn't help but smile. Clara had adopted Adeline's way of referring to everything magical as "witchy business". Her cousin had thought it was funny at first, having grown up in the magical world, but she seemed to be enjoying Adeline's slightly tongue-in-cheek way of referring to it.

"Do you think the photo of his father caused the problem?" Adeline asked. "Like he wasn't supposed to be included in the spell, but got roped in because of that?"

"Could well be. If the spell was cast on his father and Mimi's nan while they were alive, and then they both died soon after, they could have taken it with them, as it were."

That made sense. Adeline's magic was about as far from an exact science as you could get, coming more from instinct than formal process. She could see how the smallest changes could have unexpected consequences.

"I don't know what system of magic Hadley's using," Clara continued, "but if it's a power that doesn't really belong to him, it might be unstable."

"So how do we reverse it?" Adeline's frustration at the situation rose up again. "I pulled all the paper out, but it didn't change anything."

"I wouldn't be too sure of that." Adeline heard the smile in Clara's voice. "You, Mimi, and Hemi all sound like you're communicating a lot better than you were. That's the start of the spell unravelling."

Adeline couldn't deny that was true. Something had shifted for all of them. She felt connected again, not just to Hemi and Mimi, but to herself. "But I still can't talk to the ghosts."

"That bit might be more complicated. You might have to recreate the link."

Adeline would have to think on that. She knew she

couldn't rush it. Finding the right action to enhance her magic took time.

"What about Hadley?" she asked.

Clara made a noise in her throat. "It would help if we could figure out where his power is coming from. What's his surname?"

"I don't know. Hold on a sec." Adeline walked back into the kitchen.

"Mimi, what's Hadley's surname?"

Mimi looked up, surprised. She was standing in front of the stove now, and her cheeks had flushed a pretty pink from the heat. "Brackenridge. Why?"

"Ask her if he has any living relatives."

"Does he have any other relatives?" Adeline repeated. She put Clara on speakerphone so she wouldn't have to keep parroting everything Clara said. Adeline placed the phone on the counter, and she leaned in, listening as Mimi and Clara spoke. This wasn't quite as good as having Clara over for dinner, but at least the cousins were finally meeting each other.

Mimi thought for a moment. "He talked about an aunt," she said finally. "Great-aunt Hester, I think she was. He said something about visiting her in Wellington. She was staying somewhere… it had a weird name like Raven's Home or—"

"Oh, do you mean Raven's Haven?" asked Clara.

"Could be. Is that a retirement village?"

Clara chuckled. "Kind of. It's where we send the badly behaved witches. Raven's Haven for Women of Magic."

Adeline couldn't help but laugh herself. A home for badly behaved witches sounded like a disaster waiting to happen. "Could you go visit? Is it like the magical supplies shop where you have to know it's there to be able to find it?"

"Sort of, but yes, absolutely. I'll pop over tonight and see if Hester will talk to me. I'll call you back if I find out anything useful."

By the time they finished dinner, Adeline had formulated a plan. Well, perhaps "plan" was putting too fine a point on it. Plans required steps and details and knowing exactly what you're supposed to do. Adeline had none of those things, but she had the essence of what they needed to enable the ghosts to be able to talk to her and Mimi. That was more than they'd had recently, and she couldn't help feeling excited by it.

"The ghosts stopped being able to talk to Nana Tui when Hadley cut off sound," she told Mimi and Hemi. "Symbolically, I mean, through the windchimes."

Hemi nodded. "We're with you so far."

Adeline couldn't help but feel he was teasing her a little. He often didn't understand her ghost plans. Most of the time, he couldn't see what was happening, but he was always willing to go along with her, and she loved him for it.

"We still don't think he was trying to stop the ghosts talking, though, right?" Mimi asked.

"No, I think it was about your nan – trying to stop her telling you not to date him."

If Hadley's father had been friends with Nana Tui, perhaps he hadn't wanted his son to date Mimi either. He had to have known, or at least suspected, what his son was like, and perhaps felt protective towards Mimi.

"So, the idea is that we find a way to 'hear' the ghosts even though they can't hear us. Like we touch the same things they touch... move the same things they move. I think that will reverse the spell."

Mimi and Hemi both nodded, but they didn't say anything, clearly unimpressed with the idea.

"So... we just wait till they show up?" Hemi said eventually, obviously realising there wasn't going to be any more explanation forthcoming.

"Yeah." That should be the easiest part of Adeline's plan.

"Is there anything we can do to make them appear?" Hemi asked.

Adeline shook her head. "It all seems pretty random. I mean... I guess they appeared more often when Hadley was around."

Mimi sighed. "Maybe I should just call him. Forget about the ghosts, just face him and get this over with."

As if waiting for that cue, swirls of smoke appeared in the room. Adeline should have thought of that earlier. If they really were trying to keep Mimi away from Hadley, of course they would appear when she threatened to go see him.

The smoky wisps started to take shape. The man with the moustache – Hadley's father – appeared, along with the familiar faceless ghosts.

"Showtime," Adeline said. Mimi and Hemi both sat up. Of course, they couldn't see the ghosts, but they stared into the air, following Adeline's eyeline as if they could. The other ghosts remained faceless, and Adeline tried not to look at them.

"What do we do?" Mimi whispered.

Adeline reached out a hand to Mimi, beckoning her over. Mimi glanced between Adeline and the empty air where the ghosts stood, then darted over to Adeline as if she was trying to move without them noticing her. She gripped Adeline's hand when she reached her.

Adeline squeezed her fingers. "I'm going to guide you, okay?"

Mimi nodded, though she looked terrified at the prospect.

Adeline moved slowly forward, pulling Mimi with her. "They can't see me, but they can see you. We're going to try and make it clear to them that we know where they are – that we're acknowledging them, and the warning they've been trying to give you about Hadley."

"But I *can't* see them."

"That doesn't mean you can't interact."

The ghost touched the back of the couch, and Adeline pushed Mimi's hand, brushing the same spot. If the ghost noticed this, he didn't show it. He continued floating around the room, stopping near the piano.

"Wait, the piano!" Adeline pulled Mimi over. One of the ghosts had played the same notes Mimi had on the piano back at home, repeating them in a chord. Adeline pressed down a key. The ghost didn't react, but Adeline wasn't expecting him to. "Yesterday, after you touched the piano, the ghost did too. This might work!" She gestured for Mimi to give it a try.

Mimi pressed down the same note Adeline had, but hesitantly, the sound coming out softer. At least it was in tune this time. They paused, waiting. The ghosts seem to think about this. Adeline was close enough to see the swirling smoke move in Hadley's father's irises.

One of the faceless ghosts stepped forward, her finger landing on the same key Mimi had just played. She pressed it lightly, the note only just audible.

Adeline let out a breath. "It's working."

Mimi tried again and this time, Hadley's father pressed the key she'd touched, the sound louder. Mimi let out a surprised giggle as the note rang out through the room. Adeline could swear the ghosts looked pleased, recognising that they were being acknowledged. They tried a few more times, playing out a little tune which the ghosts repeated back.

Adeline held up a finger, gesturing for Mimi to pause. She touched the key herself, playing a single note. The ghosts hesitated, and Adeline held her breath. Then they played the note back.

"Yes!" The ghosts were acknowledging Adeline, even if not directly. She was getting closer to breaking the spell. "Okay, we're getting somewhere."

As if he had heard her and didn't like the sentiment, the ghost suddenly lunged forward. Adeline let out a scream, despite herself, as the ghost's fingers brushed Mimi's neck. She yanked Mimi back, wrapping her arms around her and cowering over her.

Hemi shot up from his seat. "What is it? What happened?"

Adeline peered out, but the ghosts were gone. She sighed, releasing Mimi from the stranglehold she had on her.

"He just lunged at Mimi, tried to grab her neck." She shook her head, defeated. "I thought we were getting somewhere."

Hemi touched her arm, gently rubbing it. "It was a good idea. It was worth a shot."

Adeline's phone rang, and she screamed again. Mimi and Hemi both grabbed her just as startled as she was. They all broke into giggles. She should have put her phone on silent.

"It'll be Clara." Adeline picked up the phone, answering it. "Hello?"

"Hey, it's me," Clara said. "Any progress?"

"Barely. Did you find out anything at Raven's Haven?"

"Maybe." Clara sounded hesitant, but Adeline knew her cousin wouldn't be mentioning it if there wasn't at least a possibility she'd found something significant. Adeline put the phone on speaker.

"I met Hester," Clara continued. "She said she fell out with Hadley a long time ago. He never had very strong magic, and he was always pushing Hester to share hers. She didn't want to, because she didn't like the way he was behaving."

Well, that could explain why Hadley had such strong power now. "Is that possible? To share power like that?"

"Their magic is really different to ours, so I don't know. He ended up stealing some things from her, so she thinks he might have taken it that way."

"What sort of things?" Mimi asked.

"Hester wasn't exactly sure, because it was all little things. He did it slowly, a few bits at a time, so at first, she didn't notice. Mostly it was little knickknacks, books, things that he thought might have been significant to her. He also took some money and some jewellery, but she thought he might have sold that."

"Jewellery…" Mimi's hand moved suddenly to her neck. At first, Adeline thought she was reacting to where the ghost had tried to grab her, but then her hand closed around her necklace.

"He gave me this." Mimi pulled the chain from her neck with a jerk. Could the ghost have been trying to take it from her? Now that Adeline thought about it, he had lunged for Mimi's neck several times. Had it all been about the necklace?

Mimi stared at it, shaking her head. "I don't want anything of his, but I forgot I was even still wearing it."

That couldn't be a coincidence. There must be magic in it to encourage Mimi to keep the necklace on, or at least to forget about it – just like the windchime.

Adeline held out her hand. "Give it to me, quickly."

Mimi gave her the necklace, and Adeline closed it in her palm. She could feel the power coming off it – heavy, unpleasant, pulsing magic.

"He said it was a family heirloom," Mimi whispered.

And it probably was, Adeline thought, just not one Hadley had legally inherited. "Mimi, go and find anything Hadley gave you – anything that could have belonged to Hester."

"I'll help," Hemi said. They raced upstairs, searching the house for things that Hadley could have left there.

"Adeline, hold on one second," Clara said, then a new voice came on the phone line – Hester, Adeline presumed.

"The necklace…" Hester said. "What does it look like?"

Adeline cautiously opened her hand, hoping none of the power would slip out. "It's a large pendant with a bluey-green stone in the middle." The stone seemed to change colour as she looked at it, shifting unnaturally. "It's got a silver setting with swirls carved around it."

Hester clicked her tongue. "Damn that boy!"

Adeline got the feeling Hester would have quite liked to say something much harsher there.

"It's a locket," Hester said. "That necklace has been in

our family for generations. It's probably imbued with all of our power."

"A locket?" Adeline asked. The pendant didn't look like it could open. "Would Hadley have known that?"

"I showed him how to open it when he was little." Hester clucked her tongue again. "Trace the pattern on the back. You'll find a tiny catch."

Adeline ran her hands down the swirls. It reminded her of the swirling pattern on the windchimes. "Did Hadley also steal a windchime from you by any chance?" she asked Hester.

Hester gave a little gasp. "I knew it didn't blow away! That little bugger."

Adeline cursed herself for rescuing the chime from the trash. She should have let Mimi throw it out when she'd wanted to, instead of letting it lurk, forgotten, in the back garden, its nasty spell seeping out over all of them.

Upstairs, Mimi and Hemi's footsteps thudded on the floor, as they raced from room to room, calling to each other as they found things out of place. No wonder Hadley's power over Mimi had been so strong.

Adeline traced her finger along the locket's pattern. She felt the tiniest little bump on the back and pressed it. Adeline pulled the two halves of the locket apart. Inside was a piece of paper. She pulled it out and unfolded it. Hadley had written his and Mimi's names with a heart drawn around them, just like something out of a primary school notebook. Underneath it were the words "You love me. No one else can tell you otherwise."

"It wasn't just the windchimes," she told Clara and Hester. "He had another spell inside the locket."

"Quickly, Adeline," Clara's voice came through the speaker. "Whatever you were doing to repair the link between you and the ghosts – try it again now while the power's strong."

Adeline dropped the necklace, rushing back over to the piano. She picked out a tune, childhood lessons coming back to her. One of the faceless ghosts appeared next to her, Hadley's father taking shape on her other side.

"Come on," she whispered. "You can hear me; I know you can."

Their hands joined hers on the keyboard, at first repeating the notes she played, and then picking out their own tunes, joining her in a stilted duet.

Adeline heard a sharp intake of breath beside her, and she turned to look. The faceless ghost was no longer faceless.

"You did it, Adeline. You saved her," said Nana Tui.

part of Adeline had been expecting Mimi to be able to see the ghosts, once Hadley's influence had been stripped away. She couldn't. She and Hemi came running back downstairs at Adeline's shout but passed straight through the smoky outlines of their ancestors. There were tears anyway, accompanied by many ghostly hugs and words of love spoken and then passed on by Adeline.

"I'm so sorry, Nana Tui," Mimi kept saying. "I'm so sorry."

Eventually, Nana Tui stopped asking Adeline to pass on that she didn't in any way blame Mimi for what had happened. Instead, she just laid the ghostly outlines of her hands on the sides of Mimi's face and pressed her forehead to Mimi's. Mimi grew still, feeling the forgiveness, even if she couldn't hear it.

"Now," Nana Tui said eventually. "Let's get that boy of yours sorted, Jeffry."

Hadley's father grimaced. "Honestly, if I still had hands, I'd be slapping him on the side of the head right now."

The ghosts circled around Mimi, offering their protection as she called Hadley, asking him to come over. They had faces now, but Adeline didn't recognise most of them. She suspected Mimi and Hemi might not either, even if they'd been able to see them. Nana Tui had called ancestors from generations back, all of them coming to protect Mimi from the danger Hadley posed. Adeline could see Mimi felt it – growing stronger, as she drew her family around her. Even her voice on the phone to Hadley was more powerful than Adeline had ever heard it.

"Tui, I don't mean to interrupt," Hadley's father touched Nana Tui's arm, the smoke of their outlines intermingling as he did, "but I believe my wayward son is nearly here."

They all heard the car pull up outside, and it was almost as if their heads all turned as one to look. Coco leapt up running to the door and peering out. He looked back at Adeline, waiting for her to open the door to let him run out to greet the visitor, but Adeline shook her head.

"No, puppy. Mimi needs to do this one on her own."

"We'll all be here, though," Hadley's father said. "If she needs us."

Mimi took a shaky breath. Her face paled and it was

clear the thought of doing it on her own terrified her, but Jeffry was right. She wouldn't really be on her own. Adeline and Hemi, Coco, Jeffry, and Nana Tui, along with all of the ghosts… They would all be with her.

"You can do this," Adeline told her." She took Mimi's hand, squeezing it briefly before releasing it. Mimi looked to Hemi, and he nodded. Adeline could see it was taking everything in him not to rush outside and deal with Hadley himself, but he knew just as well as Adeline did that Mimi needed to do this for herself.

"Okay," Mimi said.

"We'll be right here. Just call if you need us to come out." Hemi squeezed her shoulder.

Mimi gave a grim smile. "I won't."

Mimi walked out onto the porch. Her hair flew behind her in the breeze, and she stood, tall, fierce, strong woman that she'd always been. Hadley hadn't taken any of that power from her. He might have squashed it down for a while – frightened it into submission – but he could never truly take her strength. The ghosts of her ancestors lined up behind her, Nana Tui and Jeffry taking places on either side of her.

Hadley got out of the car. He took a few steps towards Mimi, trademark charming smile fixed on his face. It faltered as he saw Mimi, her power undeniable.

"I don't want you here, Hadley," she told him. She said it simply, no anger or theatrics.

Adeline and Hemi stayed inside, letting Mimi face him

on her own, but the ghosts stood around Mimi, lending her their strength.

"Babe, you don't mean that." Hadley sent out a wave of magic. Even from inside, Adeline felt it trying to wrap threads around her, but his magic relied on Mimi feeling weak. She wasn't a witch, but her own innate, human power shined through when she felt confident in herself. He was no match for her now.

"I said: I want you to leave. I know what you did. You put those bones in the yard. You made me think I was crazy. You don't deserve me. You need to leave, and never come back."

Hadley's smile faltered. His eyes flicked to the empty space above the porch where the windchimes had been, and fear grew on his face.

"It's over, son," Jeffry said. His voice was whispery, easy to mistake for the wind, but there was power behind it. "You need to leave her alone."

Hadley didn't hear the voice, but he felt the breeze that came with it, and the magic driving it. He sent a wave of his own back, threads wrapping around Mimi. This time it was stronger, and Mimi involuntarily took a step towards him. Nana Tui reached out a hand, gripping Mimi's between her transparent fingers.

"It's just the wind," Adeline whispered. "He's nothing but the wind.

The breeze turned to gusts. Hadley's anger grew, and with that, his power. "How can you say that to me?" he yelled.

"After everything I've done for you… you would be nothing without me. You'd be crying on the floor over some stupid bird." His magic rose up, wind whipping around Mimi.

Coco whimpered. He pawed at the door, and Adeline moved to stand beside him, but she didn't open it. Mimi would tell her if she needed them out there.

"It's just the wind," Adeline said again, her voice rising, magic fighting Hadley's. "He is nothing but the wind." She drew on her own ancestors, and on Hemi's too, both their families drawing together to push back Hadley's unwelcome power. She felt Jeffry join them, and Clara and Hester all the way from Wellington. All of them wrapped Mimi in love, and strength, forcing Hadley away.

Suddenly, everything grew still. Hadley took a step back, and then another. "Stupid cow," he said. "You have no idea what you've just thrown away." His words were angry, but there was no power in them. His magic was gone, taken back by Hester and his father. Jeffry followed him, matching him step for step, making sure he actually left. He got in his car; Jeffry slipped straight through the door to join him as he drove away.

Adeline and Hemi opened the front door, rushing out onto the porch to join Mimi. Coco bounded out too, and Mimi dropped into a crouch, letting him lick her face.

"Is it over?" Mimi asked.

Adeline nodded. "Yes, his power over you is gone. We'll package up the necklace, and anything else you found, and take it back to Hester at Raven's Haven. She'll be able to get rid of any remaining magic."

Mimi closed her eyes, her whole body relaxing with the relief.

Nana Tui clucked her tongue. She gathered herself up as if she was getting ready to go out for the evening. Adeline's stomach dropped. Perhaps she was. Now this was all over, she had no reason to stick around, haunting Mimi.

"Now, bub," she said. "Before I get on going, you tell me, what's all this about selling the house?"

Adeline repeated Nana Tui's question, and Mimi shrunk a little. She looked between Adeline and the empty air where she knew Nana Tui stood. "I thought that would be fair… If I sell it, I could split the money between all the grandkids. You only left the house to me because I came to stay with you when you were sick, but I did such a terrible job of looking after you, and…"

Adeline suddenly understood Mimi's discomfort with the house, and with talking about caring for Nana Tui in her final days. She felt she'd been given the house under false pretences, unable to save her nana from her inevitable fate.

Nana Tui clucked her tongue. "Adeline, you tell that girl she's talking nonsense. I was an old woman. There was no saving me from the grave. Besides," she gave a cheeky grin. "I didn't leave her the house because she took care of me. I did it because she's my favourite."

Adeline relayed this message, and Mimi and Hemi both laughed. Hemi put his arm around her. "It's true. She loved you so much, cuz."

Nana Tui nodded. "Still do."

Nana Tui was starting to fade, and Adeline's eyes began to well. Even though they couldn't see it, Mimi and Hemi seemed to sense their ancestors were leaving. They pulled close together, drawing Adeline into a hug too.

"Goodbye, Nana Tui," Mimi whispered.

"We miss you," Hemi said, through tears. "We love you so much."

Nana Tui placed a hand on each of their cheeks in turn, then she stepped towards Adeline. "You're going to be a great mum, child, don't you worry about that. Nana Tui knows these things." She touched Adeline's stomach gently, and Bump kicked as if in response.

"Thank you," Adeline whispered.

And then she was gone.

Mimi and Hemi drew in even closer, and Coco squished his way in between their feet, wanting to be a part of the hug. Suddenly, Adeline couldn't wait to go visit Hemi's mum and to tell her all about her grandchild. She couldn't wait to get home and tell Clara, Dana, and all of their friends.

The ancestors disappeared from around them, but not really. Adeline could still feel them nearby. She could feel the connection running through the years, through her and Hemi, and this magical new baby growing inside her.

The End.

A NOTE FROM HELEN VIVIENNE FLETCHER

Hello! I hope you enjoyed *Curses and Cousins*. I first wrote about Adeline, Coco and Hemi in *Familiars and Foes*. I loved writing about them so much, I just had to continue their story a sequel.

If you liked *Curses and Cousins*, please consider reviewing it on Amazon or Goodreads. Every review helps!

Want more witchy fiction? Keep reading for a list of all the Witchy Fiction books written by my friends and I here in New Zealand. If you'd like to find out more about us and our books, check out our website at www.witchyfiction.com or find us on Facebook.

ABOUT THE AUTHOR

Helen Vivienne Fletcher is a widely published children's and young adult author, storyteller and award-winning playwright. She has written an impressive collection of work for everyone from pre-schoolers to adult readers. Spanning a variety of subjects, Helen's writing doesn't shy away from the gritty parts of life. Diving into the depths of disability, the gravitas of grief or the thrill of the mysterious, her stories are sublimely suspenseful whether on the page or stage. Connecting the real world with flights of fantasy, she creates fast-paced fiction to delight and draw in readers and audiences across Aotearoa.

She lives in Wellington with her disability assistance dog, Bindi – a five-year-old, playful Labrador who loves soft toys, cuddles, and can fit three tennis balls in her mouth at once.

Overall, Helen just loves telling stories and is always excited when people want to read or hear them.

Find out more at www.helenvfletcher.com.

MORE WITCHY FICTION BOOKS

Need more witchy goodness in your life? Check out the full list of Witchy Fiction books below!

Succulents and Spells (Windflower One) by Andi C. Buchanan: Laurel Windflower is a witch from a family of magic workers - but her own life is going nowhere until Marigold Nightfield knocks on her door. Marigold is a scientist from a family of witches, and she's in search of monsters. What lies ahead could reveal all Laurel's shortcomings to the woman she's trying to impress... or uncover the true nature of her power.

Hexes & Vexes by Nova Blake: Small towns are full of gossip, and Mia is pretty sure that no one in her hometown of Okato has ever stopped talking about her. Cast off by her best friend, blamed for a local tragedy – Mia had no choice but to run away.

Now, ten years later, she's being dragged back.

Brand of Magic (Redferne Witches, Book One) by K M Jackways: Hazel Redferne is an empath witch but she's given up on magic. When her neighbour, Joel, needs her marketing expertise, Hazel jumps right in to help. But an attack on her powerful aunt means unlocking her psychic powers is the key to protecting the Redferne witches. Can Hazel let magic - and love - back in?

Witching with Dolphins by Janna Ruth: Friends before magic (or boys) has always been Harper's prerogative. Her best friend Valerie is everything she is not: beautiful, confident, and the most powerful witch on Banks Peninsula. They might not see eye to eye on everything, yet, when a sinister scientist threatens their coven, Harper is willing to give up everything: the man they both love, her life, or even the little magic she has.

Holloway Witches by Isa Pearl Ritchie: Ursula escapes to Holloway Road leaving her former life in tatters following a bad break-up. She's looking forward to a quiet respite in a cozy cottage with a lush garden and lots of bookshelves, but instead she can't shake the eerie feeling she's being followed...

Familiars and Foes (Familiar Magic Book One) by Helen Vivienne Fletcher: Adeline yearns for family, but for years, the closest she's gotten is her assistance dog, Coco. When a frightening encounter with a ghost brings an old friend back into her life, it seems like Adeline's about to find the companionship she's been missing. But her crush might have to wait. As the ghost's smoky presence increases, Adeline feels its hold on those around her tightening dangerously.

Overdues and Occultism by Jamie Sands: That Basil is a librarian comes as no surprise to his Mt Eden community. That he's a witch? Yeah. That might raise more than a few eyebrows. When Sebastian, a paranormal investigator filming a web series starts snooping around Basil's library, he stirs up more than just Basil's heart.

Riverwitch by Rem Wigmore: Self-taught witch Ashley Robinson spends most of her time on community work and picking up litter. When something goes badly wrong with the Waikato River, Ash is determined to get to the bottom of it. If only Bryony Manu, the other witch in town, could put aside their arrogance to help.

Jingle Spells: A mysterious child is spotted swimming far from the beach. A woman searches for a ghost in a blacked-out hospital. One witch introduces her lover to her family, while another takes care of a magicaholic baby dolphin in her boyfriend's absence. A young man bonds with his pet eel, and yarnbombers accidentally summon something otherworldly. Jingle Spells is a collection of fun, quirky, and witchily magical Christmas stories by seven Witchy Fiction authors.

Microscopes and Magic (Windflower Two) by Andi C. Buchanan: Marigold Nightfield's life changed when she absorbed the magic stored in a family heirloom. Now, she's part of a growing network of magic-working scientists who are trying to change the world for the better, and has a girlfriend from a sprawling, powerful, witchy family. But when her girlfriend's work is destroyed by possible sabotage, and strange things start appearing in Wellington's green belt, Marigold's amazing new life starts to unravel. She'll have to not only draw on her scientific background and magical abilities, but make new connections and grow in confidence to face this new threat.

A Gap in the Veil by Sam Schenk: As a mechanic, Greg can fix just about anything—except his broken heart. When a visiting musician dials up the charm after a gig in town, Greg's life looks to be taking a turn for the better. His plans to keep things simple between them are complicated by the awakening of a spirit bent on corruption. Greg must make choices between appearing distant or bringing his new friend into the fight, all the while saving Wellington from a past it had almost forgotten.

Raven's Haven for Women of Magic by Anna Kirtlan: Cassandra Frost has zero interest in fortune-telling or brewing foul-smelling things in cauldrons, and much prefers the company of non-magical folk. She does her best to keep her powers under wraps to protect the secrecy of the Wellington witching community. But that's easier said than done when your grandmother lives in Raven's Haven for Women of Magic. Magical fireworks, mobility broom races and irresponsible use of cat litter spells are all part of the game for the witching retirement village residents. When Cassandra's forced to cast a spell in the open to save Adrian, a geeky graphic designer with secrets of his own, her two worlds spectacularly collide, and she learns the Haven is much more than meets the eye.

Against the Grain by Melanie Harding-Shaw: After another casual fling goes horribly wrong, coeliac witch Trinity moves down the country to start over, yet again, in the bush-clad suburb of Karori. But her fresh start takes a dark turn when she discovers something is trapping her demon familiar, Saifa, in the suburb. If Trinity can't find and break the anchors of his invisible cage, she could lose everything—her power, her freedom, and her only friend in the world.

Monsters and Manuscripts by Jamie Sands One Witch, One Paranormal Investigator, and Something that went bump in the night...Library witch Basil and YouTuber Sebastian have settled into life together in the sleepy suburb of Mt Eden. Basil is overjoyed to have a handsome boyfriend to come home to and he is connecting deeper with his magic. But when strange books start to turn up at his library and an uninvited guest makes noises in their attic, it's up to them to investigate.

As a paranormal YouTuber, Sebastian can't resist a new mystery. Especially since he's been in one place for far too long… Is his enthusiasm for the next story going to ruin everything?

put Kelsey's boyfriend in a coma. The worst part? She asked him to do it.

Underwater by Helen Vivienne Fletcher: Bailey has a lot of secrets and a lot of scars, both of which she'd like to keep hidden. Unfortunately, Pine Hills Resort isn't the kind of place where anyone can keep anything hidden for long.